I'LL BE HOME FOR CHRISTMAS

A Coming Home Novella

JESSICA SCOTT

Thirty One Fox Books

"Buy it. Read it. Have lots of Kleenex on hand. Scott's stories are always powerful and emotional but they're honest, she doesn't jerk you around or manipulate you. The power of the stories and of the characters emotions gets into you and sweeps you away." - Bea's Book Nook

Meet the lovable smart ass who can always crack a joke and the woman who loves him more than life itself.

Vic Carponti always has a joke — no matter how bleak the situation might be. He's the guy who can make jokes in the middle of a firefight in Baghdad or when he's getting sewn back up after getting blown up. But his sense of humor hides a fierce loyalty to the men he serves with and a devotion to his wife who he loves more than life itself. But there's nothing funny about war...

But as he prepares to leave on his latest deployment into the violent throes of the Surge in Iraq, his jokes don't seem as funny to his wife. Nicole forces herself to laugh at his redeployment antics but behind her laughter hides the darkest fear of every Army wife — that the knock on the door may be the news that destroys her world.

They both try to make the best of the deployment but when the phone doesn't ring for a few days, Nicole starts to worry. And when the dreaded call comes telling her he's been hurt, she'll move heaven and earth to be there when her husband wakes up.

"I won't spoil it, but it will give you hope, laughter and tears!" ~ Romancing Rakes

THE COMING HOME SERIES
Because of You
I'll Be Home for Christmas: A Coming Home Novella
Anything For You: A Coming Home Short Story
Back to You
Come Home to Me: A Coming Home Novella*
Carry Me Home*
A Place Called Home*
Take Me Home*
Homefront
After The War
Last One Home*

Learn More At…
http://www.jessicascott.net
Follow Jessica on Twitter
Like Jessica on Facebook
Sign up for Jessica's Newsletter

Author's Note
The Coming Home series and Homefront series were originally published as separate series. I have rebranded them to get things organized as they were originally intended.

Come Home to Me: A Coming Home Novella* was originally published as part of the Homefront series

Carry Me Home* was originally published as **Until There Was You** as part of the Coming Home series

A Place Called Home* was originally published as **All for You** as part of the Coming Home series

Take Me Home* was originally published as **It's Always Been You** as part of the Coming Home series

Last One Home* was originally published as **Find My Way Home** as part of the Homefront series

BOOKSHOTS

Dawn's Early Light

Author's Note

The Coming Home series and Homefront series were originally published as separate series. I have rebranded them to get things organized as they were originally intended.

Come Home to Me: A Coming Home Novella* was originally published as part of the Homefront series

Carry Me Home* was originally published as Until There Was You as part of the Coming Home series

A Place Called Home* was originally published as All for You as part of the Coming Home series

Take Me Home* was originally published as It's Always Been You as part of the Coming Home series

Last One Home* was originally published as Find My Way Home as part of the Homefront series

To Donna
Because these books wouldn't be here without you.

❦ I ❦

Fort Hood, Texas
Early 2007

Sergeant Vic Carponti paused outside his company operations office, taking a deep breath. It was funny how their corner of Fort Hood felt deserted the night before a deployment. The company colors had already been cased. They would uncase them in a few weeks, once they got settled into their new home across the ocean in the middle of the war.

He didn't know why this deployment was bothering him so much. It wasn't his first time heading off to war, so he knew what to expect when the shit hit the fan in combat. But there was something hanging over his head this time. A fear that maybe this time his luck would run out.

He sighed and rubbed his face with both hands before walking into the company ops. The only thing they'd left up was the plaque that bore the names of their fallen brothers from the last deployment. The commander—Captain Trent Davila, a man Carponti had known for years—was planning on carrying that with him personally so it couldn't ever get lost.

And so no one would ever forget. Carponti reached up and took it gently off the wall, then strolled into his company commander's office with a nonchalance painted on his face that he damn sure didn't feel. But people expected him to laugh and joke and make them forget the bad shit all around and so that's what he was going to do.

"Don't forget this," he said, placing the plaque on Trent's desk. He plopped down in a chair, then kicked his feet up on Trent's desk. "Are you coming out with us tonight?"

Captain Trent Davila lifted one eyebrow at Carponti's feet and said nothing. Carponti looked at his commander and longtime friend, then at the plaque next to his boots.

"Fine," he said with a sigh, dropping his feet to the floor. "So answer the question."

Trent sighed. "I can't go out with you guys. I'm the company commander. I'm not allowed to have fun," Trent grumbled. "Besides, my boss would have my nuts in a sling if anything happens while I'm there."

"It's the last day before our deployment. You're allowed to have fun. You can just say you're supervising all of us miscreants." Carponti took the last Dr. Pepper out of Trent's fridge. "The deployment hasn't even started and you already look stressed the hell out. You should be working your lieutenant to death instead of trying to do everything yourself."

Trent shook his head and pushed his glasses to

the top of his head. "Yeah, well, my new executive officer seems to think he's God's gift to the Army. He's good but he's not as good as he thinks he is."

"Oh, the boys just love him," Carponti said.

"Really?"

"No, not really. He's an arrogant fuck who believes his own press. Personally, I can't stand him, but luckily I don't have to deal with him much. I just sic Sarn't Garrison on him."

Trent grinned and reached for the plaque, sliding his hat on top of it so he wouldn't forget it. "Yeah, Garrison has a way with words."

Garrison was Carponti's platoon sergeant. Garrison and Trent had been squad leaders many moons ago when Trent had still been enlisted. In Carponti's world, it meant a whole lot that Trent had stayed close with his enlisted friends even after he'd crossed over to the dark side and become an officer.

"I'm swinging by his place on my way home. He needs to go out before someone shoots his grumpy old ass. He's been a complete buzz kill since his wife left him."

"Your sympathy is astounding," Trent said dryly. He grinned and shook his head. "Why do we put up with you?"

"Because I'm charming and funny and good in a firefight?" Carponti said with a grin.

"Pretty much. You can make anyone laugh."

"It's an important life skill. Like balancing a checkbook. So seriously, find a babysitter and come out with us. Your wife could use some fun before she has to spend the year dealing with all the spouses in the Family Readiness Group and chasing your kids around while you're off on another fun adventure."

"I wouldn't exactly call going to combat a fun adventure." Trent rubbed his chest. There was a scar there, Carponti knew. A scar that had damn near killed Trent several years ago. Carponti wondered just how much stress his commander was carrying and not telling anyone. Trent's face flushed when he realized Carponti had caught him rubbing his scar and he tapped the pencil hard enough to snap the eraser off. "You know, you're right. Let me see if we can't find a sitter."

"Excellent. We'll be congregating by the bar when you get there. Now I just have to go convince Garrison to come out with us."

"Good luck with that," Trent said, pulling his glasses down. "He's on the verge of becoming a warrior monk."

"Not if I have anything to say about it," Carponti mumbled as he strolled out of his commander's office. He wished he hadn't seen the flicker of worry that flashed in his commander's eyes when he'd mentioned his wife. He'd thought that Laura and Trent were one of the strongest couples he knew. She'd put up with him deploying back to back to back since he'd almost died a few years ago.

But that flicker of worry? Yeah, Carponti hadn't missed it. There were problems there, hopefully small ones that Trent would take time to fix after this rotation into the sandbox.

Carponti looked down at his own wedding ring. It was his last night home and his last night with his wife.

He was glad he'd convinced her to come out with him and the boys. That way he could make sure they had a most excellent party and spend time with

Nicole at the same time. He was going to spend part of the night chaperoning his guys to make sure they made the most of it— which meant making sure no one ended up in jail—but then? Then the time he had left was going to be spent making his wife laugh.

Because try though he might, he couldn't shake the quiet dread that settled in the pit of his stomach that tonight was the last night of normalcy he had on this earth.

NICOLE CARPONTI BREATHED DEEPLY AND FANNED HER eyes, trying to stop the burning of hot tears. She leaned against the wall of the bathroom in *Ropers* and tried to stuff down all the churning emotions chained to the fact that her husband was leaving for war tomorrow. Again.

The first time he'd left she'd been scared, but then the war, the deployment...the waiting...it had all been unknown. She'd worked on finishing her degree and kept herself busy and waited by the phone like all the military wives who had gone before her.

The second time he'd left, she'd known better what to expect. The long waits between phone calls. The silence when he couldn't talk long. The quick e-mails saying "I'm alive" that once upon a time would have been too little, but during the war were more than enough to keep her going.

But this time? This time was different. The Surge was different. They were sending in massive amounts of soldiers to try to quell the Iraqi insurgency. It was bloody and deadly and soldiers were getting attacked at higher rates than at any earlier time during the war.

And Nicole was terrified.

She had to hide it, though. She'd agreed to come out with him tonight just because it gave her a chance to pretend that she was fine. She had to keep everything in check until after he left. She couldn't let him know how much she worried this time.

Fanning her eyes once more, she stepped out of the bathroom and into the rowdy country bar. A place like this was guaranteed trouble on a normal night, but tonight her husband's platoon was rolling deep. Which was either going to be a really good thing or a really bad thing for her future job at the Army's Criminal Investigation Division, depending on how cantankerous tonight got.

She spotted her good friend Laura Davila at the bar with a cute blond woman Nicole had met in the bathroom a little while ago. She had already completely forgotten the other woman's name. She was terrible with names.

She wound her way through the pulsating crowd until she reached them. Laura grinned at her and she exclaimed, "I can't believe you came out tonight."

"You've already said this twice," Laura said. They had to shout to hear each other.

Nicole flagged down the bartender and leaned around Laura to her friend. "I'm a terrible person but I already forgot your name. I'm Nicole Carponti."

The petite blond held out her hand. "Jen St. James."

"Nice to meet you, Jen. I won't forget this time," Nicole said with a smile.

Laura leaned toward Nicole. "I'm trying to get

her out of her shell. She had cancer and she's been struggling with her self-esteem ever since."

Nicole frowned, glancing toward Jen, who was now trying to get the attention of the bartender. On the other side of her, though, was Garrison, her husband's platoon sergeant. He was a big man and he was currently leaning down to talk to Jen. "How's that for a self-esteem boost?" Nicole said, gesturing toward the two.

Laura glanced over, then quickly looked away before she was caught. Her eyes lit with a brilliant smile. "Oh, that couldn't be more perfect if I had planned it."

Nicole studied her friend through narrowed eyes. "Did you plan it?"

"I wish. But let's just see how this little situation develops, shall we?"

Nicole raised her beer in mock salute to her friend. "You, m'dear, are a devious and loyal friend."

"I'll drink to that," Laura said. "So how's Carponti taking this deployment?"

Nicole heard the undercurrent in her friend's voice. "You know how he is. Always cracking jokes, which I suppose is a good thing. I'm terrified, though."

"Yeah, I know. I've been talking to some of the spouses. The Surge has everyone terrified. One of the spouses told me it was a death sentence." Laura took a sip from her beer, scanning the bar.

Nicole scoffed quietly. "How's that for melodramatic?" But she didn't voice her own fear that this deployment was going to be worse than the previous ones. "I don't envy you as the Family Readiness Group leader."

"Oh, come on, don't you want to volunteer? You can be responsible for keeping me from going crazy. It's a primary duty position, you know."

Nicole laughed. "Not in this lifetime," she said. "I always feel out of place once the spouses find out I'm pretty much a cop."

Jen leaned over, rejoining their conversation as Garrison wandered off in the direction of Laura's husband. "What's going on over there?" she said, pointing at Laura's husband.

Nicole sighed heavily and took another drink. "Oh joy. Looks like Trent is giving one of his lieutenants some love. Couldn't have the rest of the night without drama, could we?" She glanced back at Laura and Jen. "We should go interrupt before the second round of fireworks go off."

Earlier, Vic had gotten into an argument with Lieutenant Randall and now it looked like Laura's husband was finishing things off with the arrogant prick. The LT made Nicole's skin crawl and she wasn't looking forward to another bar fight. Not two in one night, that was for sure.

But whatever had happened was over now. She watched as LT Randall made a beeline for the door. Out of the corner of her eye, she saw Garrison talking to Jen again. And Laura? Once Randall was gone, she and her husband moved off to a dark corner of the bar and were deep in conversation.

She hoped it was a good one. She didn't like the worry she'd seen in her friend's eyes when she talked about her husband.

She snuck up behind Vic, sliding her hands over his hips and up under his t-shirt and the smooth hard skin of his body, placing a kiss at the indentation between his shoulder blades.

He turned and wrapped his arms around her shoulders. "There you are." He kissed her fiercely, reminding her of how much she loved this man. "I was about to send out a search party for you in the little girls' room."

Nicole wrapped her arms around his waist and lifted her chin to meet his eyes. He was leaner than he'd been when he'd come home last year. His body was more solid from long ruck marches and hard training for this deployment. His eyes, though, were the same bright, mischievous green that they'd always been and she counted herself lucky that whatever he'd gone through in the war, he'd come home okay so far. She just prayed their luck held.

"No search party required," she murmured against his lips. "I was talking to Laura. I'm impressed that you got Garrison and Trent to come out."

"You should be," Vic grumbled, biting her bottom lip gently. "I had to guilt both of them into it. It's like they both turned thirty and amputated their fun genes or something."

Nicole laughed against his mouth. "Dance with me?" she asked.

"What in our history makes you think I know how to dance?" he grumbled even as he allowed her to lead him onto the dance floor.

"You'll figure it out," she said, sliding her arms around his neck. She rubbed her body against his, sensuously moving her hips in time with the music.

He dropped his hands to her hips, guiding her exactly where he wanted her. "Keep that up and we'll have to sneak out to the car," he said, his breath hot on her ear.

She nibbled on his bottom lip, biting it gently. "I think you're trying to seduce me," she whispered. She dug her fingers into his back, her blood humming with latent arousal. God but she loved this man.

"I'm absolutely trying to seduce you," he said. He angled his thigh between hers, pressing close to the juncture of her thighs. The pressure sent vibrations through her body and straight to her core.

"I'm kind of ready to go home." Her words were a gasp as he rubbed his thigh against her swollen center. "Before you get into any more fights with your lieutenant."

"Can we not talk about work when I'm trying to turn you on?" he mumbled. He slipped his hand beneath the hem of her shirt, stroking his thumb down the centerline of her back. A shiver ran through her.

"You don't want to talk about work? That doesn't turn you on?" She undulated against him, grateful for the crush of bodies that swayed around them and enabled them to be lost in the crowd.

"No, trying to get you naked turns me on," he said. "We really need to get out of here." His breath traced over her ear a moment before he bit her earlobe gently, a fierce burst of pleasure in the pain.

"That sounds like a brilliant idea."

He sighed as a commotion cleared a corner of the dance floor. "I hate being one of the responsible adults." He kissed her hard. "Let me get everyone out of here first? That way no one goes to jail on our last night in the States."

She kissed him fiercely. "I'll be waiting over here for you to get done being all caveman."

"I'll show you caveman later," he said with a grin before wading into the crowd and diffusing the situation between Garrison and Trent.

It took the better part of an hour before they'd shuffled everyone off to their respective cabs and vehicles. Nicole talked with Laura and Jen and tried not to notice how Jen kept watching Garrison.

It felt like forever before her husband strolled across the parking lot and scooped her up, carrying her toward their vehicle.

Their car was parked deep in a shadowed corner of the parking lot, and the moment her husband closed the door, Nicole crawled into his lap on the passenger's seat. He pulled her close, kissing her hard and fast. Pouring a thousand unsaid things into that kiss. His hand threaded into her hair and he slanted her mouth until he owned her—all of her— and she was lost in his taste, his touch.

Then he broke off abruptly. "What the hell?"

"What?"

"Who is that with Garrison?"

Nicole twisted around in time to see Garrison, one of Carponti's oldest friends, lean in to kiss Jen.

"Oh, now that's interesting," Carponti whispered.

Nicole spun around. "Don't you say anything to him," she said.

"Why not?"

"Because this is the first time Garrison has done anything for himself since his wife left him. Leave him alone."

Carponti blinked innocently. "What makes you think I would say anything?" he said. His words slurred and Nicole grinned before fishing around in his pockets for his car keys. "A little more to the left."

Nicole laughed then climbed into the driver's seat as Garrison stepped back, letting Jen walk to an ancient sedan. "She's cute. She's friends with Laura."

Laura, who was being carried across the parking lot by her husband. She hoped for Laura's sake the happiness lasted longer than just tonight. The war was taking its toll on everyone, and Nicole had noticed more than once that there was a strain in her friend's voice when she talked about her husband.

Vic just looked at her. "Oh really?"

Nicole drove them away before her husband could interrupt what had looked like something very sweet between Jen and Garrison. She'd known Garrison as long as she'd known her husband and it was long overdue for him to find someone that made him happy outside of the Army.

She glanced at her husband, who had closed his eyes the moment the vehicle started moving, a lazy smile on his lips. Something warm bloomed inside her.

She wished Garrison could find the kind of happy that she had with Vic.

❧ 2 ❧

"Hey, babe, can you find my socks?"

Nicole narrowed her eyes in the direction of the bedroom. Since the night they'd first met six years ago, she'd learned to tell when he was up to something. And he was always up to something. The man didn't know how to be serious and it was the thing she loved most about him.

But she hadn't known it that night she'd pulled him and a couple of his buddies over and arrested him. She'd been a young military police officer, eager to make a difference and her very first traffic stop at her new duty station had been a car full of smart-mouthed infantrymen, fresh out of basic training.

She'd walked up to the driver's side window and had been greeted by...a sock puppet. A sock puppet that had asked her out on a date after she'd threatened to put him in the back of the police car. Her lips curled at the memory.

Yeah, most people had romantic stories about how they met their husbands. Nicole? She had a sock puppet. She'd learned that night that when Vic's voice sounded funny, he was up to something.

And right then, standing in her living room, his socks in her hand, she paused because her husband's voice sounded a little too funny.

And that was never a good sign.

"What's wrong?" she called, stuffing his socks into the bag that would keep them protected from the desert weather.

He was deploying for the third time later today and Nicole was doing her best to stay busy, to help him pack. She was determined not to spend the last few hours she had with him crying. She'd done this all before, right? This was nothing new. Nothing different. So why did it feel like her heart was breaking in her chest? She blinked rapidly and breathed deeply. She wouldn't cry. Not today.

No, she'd save that for later, after he was gone. Today, she would laugh at his jokes because he needed her to laugh. She'd help him pack and savor the last hours she had with him.

Later, after she'd kissed him goodbye, the year would start and her countdown would begin. One day at a time, trying not to let the worry and the fear and the sadness crush her.

"Nothing's wrong. I just need you to come here for a second."

The odd catch in his voice made her instantly suspicious. Still holding the gallon bag of his t-shirts and socks she'd been packing for him, she rounded the corner into their bedroom.

And stopped short. Blinked. Then doubled over laughing.

Her husband—a decorated infantryman—stood

in the middle of their bedroom wearing her panties. And not her time-of-the-month granny panties. No, not her husband. He'd managed to squeeze into the tiny little patch of white lace.

She doubled over and clutched her sides and tried not to pee her pants.

"Oh my god. I can't breathe," she said, trying to stop laughing.

He turned around and wiggled his ass. "Does this make my butt look big?"

Nicole gasped for air. "There's something the matter with you."

"Does this get you horny, baby?" She caught the edge of shadows in his eyes despite her own tears of laughter. They were both trying so hard to laugh away the sadness of the night. She loved him even more for that. Something so simple but so important.

She swiped her fingers beneath her eyes, glad at least that she had a moment to hide the well of sadness that had surged behind the laughter. She would miss his sense of humor when he was gone. Nothing seemed as funny when Vic deployed. It was like he took funny with him every time he got on that plane. Still laughing, she crossed the small space, dropping the gallon-sized bag of t-shirts on the bed before sliding her arms around her husband's neck. "You know that you wearing my panties always gets me horny."

He pulled her close and she arched into him. He nuzzled her lips with his. "I'm not really sure what that says about you or me but I'm not going to complain."

She reached between their bodies and wound her

hand beneath the fabric, clearly not meant to contain male anatomy, and found him—flaccid.

"I think we need to get you out of these. They're inhibiting your performance," she said, hooking her thumbs in the waistband.

"I think that's an excellent plan."

He shimmied out of the panties and then surprised her by scooping her up and tossing her onto the bed.

She bounced once then opened her arms for him.

She held him close for a long moment, savoring the feel of his body on hers, knowing it was going to be the last time she would have him with her for a long while.

She knew the fear she would live with for the next year. And she hated it.

But she loved her husband and he loved being a soldier. She'd never planned on making the military a career. Vic? Vic wanted to stay forever. And because she loved him, she'd wait for him. No matter how much it hurt.

She blinked rapidly, trying to hide the tears that burned behind her eyes, and pressed her face into his neck. Her no-crying plan was failing miserably. She swiped at her eyes and tried to keep him from seeing the tears that ran down her cheeks.

⚜

CARPONTI MIGHT BE A SMART-ASS BUT THAT DIDN'T make him an idiot. His wife was crying. He hated it when she cried. It was worse because he knew it was his fault—he was leaving again. No matter how much he tried to make light of the situation, no matter how ridiculously he behaved to coax a laugh out of her, this deployment was different and everyone knew it. He shouldn't have been surprised that Nicole was having a hard time with it. Even Trent and his wife looked like they were having a hard time.

Everyone was—her, the guys, the guys' wives. Carponti and his boys were getting ready to head downrange into the Surge, a shit hole time in a shit hole war that didn't make a damn bit of sense to anyone. This war sucked.

But that didn't make saying good-bye any easier. And Nicole, God bless her, was doing her best to put on a brave and happy face. He felt her shudder beneath him and he tightened his arms around her a little more.

He didn't want her to cry. He hated it when she cried because it usually meant he'd screwed something up. He tried not to do that on a regular basis. He never wanted to give her a reason to realize that she could do better than a redheaded infantryman. Nicole was so far out of his league, every day he woke up wondering if today would be the day that the love of his life left him for someone better. The day she would stop laughing at his jokes.

Because, let's face it, he wasn't much of a catch. Scruffy redhead with a penchant for saying the first thing that came to mind, Carponti knew his weaknesses. And still, his wife, his beautiful, talented wife with a degree in criminal justice, chose him. He'd married her as fast as he could just to keep her around. Even when she'd gotten out of the Army to pursue her degree, even when she could be with someone smarter, better looking—not better in the sack, though. Carponti had always taken care of her that way. He marveled at the ways he could bring her pleasure—just like the sound of her laughter, the sound of her coming was its own special pleasure.

All because she'd pulled him over for driving like an ass and said yes to a date with a sock puppet. He was the luckiest son of a bitch on the planet.

He lifted himself on his arms and looked down at her, stroking her blond hair out of her face and cupping her cheek. Her eyes were a little bit red and she was trying to hide it and failing badly.

"Don't cry, babe," he whispered.

"I'm trying not to." She pressed her lips to his. "Sorry."

He grasped for anything to say to make her laugh and came up empty. She shifted then, her body rubbing against his, and he smiled slowly, stroking his thumb over her damp cheek.

"We are really wasting this opportunity," he said, kissing the side of her lips.

"What's that?" Her mouth curled into a faint smile, the remnants of her laugh trembling through her body.

"I'm naked. What other opportunity did you think I was talking about?"

He loved it when she laughed. Her eyes lit up and her whole face smiled. He laughed and shifted, rocking gently against her. "It's a shame you've got on so many clothes."

She lifted her arms for him as he dragged the t-shirt over her head, leaving her in a bra and her jeans. She reached between them to unhook her pants but he stopped her, his hands covering hers. He shimmied down her body. "That's my job," he whispered, then he flicked his tongue over her navel.

He loved the little sounds she made as he tugged her pants off. "Your panties look so much better on you," he said.

"I'm glad you approve." There was laughter in her voice. She threaded her fingers through his hair, her nails tracing his scalp with tiny bites of electricity.

He framed her hips in his hands and pressed his lips to her center. She arched beneath him and shifted her thighs, opening to his touch. He held her there, his thumbs holding the fabric in place when she tried to shuck out of her panties. "I want to try something."

She pushed up onto her elbows, looking down at him, a tiny frown knitted between her brows. "What, the night before you leave, now you want to get creative?"

He met her gaze, his eyes not moving from hers, and traced his tongue over the swollen mound beneath her panties.

"Oh, I am definitely going to miss your tongue when you're gone." She gasped and her breath caught in her throat. "Where on earth did you learn that trick?" she whispered.

She reached down to cradle his face in her palms and Carponti was lost for a moment in the love looking back at him. His wife, his beautiful, smart, sexy, funny wife. A tiny curl of fear licked at him. What if she got tired of waiting for him?

"I watched this sex in your marriage video with Wilks last weekend on staff duty." Nicole fell back into the bed and cracked up. "The art of making love or something. He's going through counseling with his wife and the therapist is trying to save their sex life first. So I watched it with him. See if I could pick up any pointers."

Nicole sighed and turned her head to look down at him. "You are a strange, strange man," she said, smiling. But there was a fear beneath her smile. Fear that someday, the deployments would be too much. That the distance and the time spent apart would change them. That she'd stop wanting to make love, stop loving him enough to wait for him. Garrison, Carponti's platoon sergeant, had recently gotten divorced. They both knew it was because Garrison had been gone too much.

Carponti shoved aside the melancholy, focusing instead on her body. Her touch.

"And you're wasting an opportunity to use that talented tongue of yours." She arched into him, lifting her hips in silent offering.

The laugh snuck out of him and he rested his forehead against her thigh until he could control himself. "This has got to be the corniest thing we've ever done," he said, stroking his thumb over the seam of her panties.

She scraped her nails over his cheeks, gently. "It beats spending the morning crying," she whispered.

A lump rose in his throat and he crawled up her body, capturing her face in his hands. He kissed her then, fiercely, pouring a thousand unsaid things into that one moment. He wasn't good with words or big gestures. There wasn't a way for him to tell her how much he was going to miss her. How much he worried that she would be alone, that she might go through a day without laughing because he was gone. And the unspoken fear that he would leave her alone forever. He kissed her like a dying man, peeled her clothes from her body like it was the last time he would feel her writhe beneath him—because he was terrified that it was. He paused a moment before he slid into her body, desperately grasping for something funny to say to lighten the moment, to make her laugh. But he had nothing as he fell into her embrace, sliding into her body and completing his soul.

He savored her in those final moments before her release crashed over her, shuddering through them both and taking him under with her.

"You're not serious."

Carponti turned around, his shoulders covered in flecks of red hair. "What?"

Nicole grinned as she leaned against the door. "Garrison is going to kill you."

"Garrison is going to love my new haircut. It looks just like his."

Nicole arched one blond eyebrow. "Except for the bright red fuzzy patch in the center of your head."

Carponti shrugged and rubbed his hands over his freshly shorn scalp. "I can't wait to see what the sergeant major says."

"Isn't he going to be mad?"

Carponti brushed the hair off his neck. "We're going to war. My hair isn't on the list of things he's going to worry about."

Nicole looked down at the pile of hair on the floor and sighed. "Then why do it?"

Carponti smirked. "Because it'll get a rise out of him and I live to make his blood pressure go up."

She laughed. "You need a hobby. Other than blowing things up."

He sidled across the room and hooked his thumb into the waist of her jeans and tugged her close until their hips met. "I have a hobby. Keeping you well satisfied."

She sniffed but her lips curled at the edges. "You're going to be derelict in your duties for a while."

"But I'll be home soon enough and then I'll make up for it."

"I think I'm going to need a deployment boyfriend."

He grinned wickedly. "Did you already get one?" He backed her up against the wall, his body hard against hers. God but she loved this man. "Can I see it?"

A slow flush crept over her face and she tried to look away. He threaded his fingers with hers and lifted her arms over her head. Her back arched with the movement.

"Please?" he whispered against her lips. "That would be an awesome memory to take with me downrange. Just think of me, alone in the middle of the desert. One visual of you with your deployment boyfriend and it could make a lonely night go by so much faster."

Nicole giggled until the laugh overwhelmed her and she was gasping for air. He released her hands and she threaded them around his neck. She buried her face against his throat and laughed.

"There's something really wrong with you," she

said when she could breathe again. "I'll send you a video."

He brightened instantly. "Really?"

"Yes. And dirty letters."

"Promise?" He nibbled along the edge of her jaw, guiding her slowly backward toward their bed, stacked high with his two duffle bags and all the crap he still hadn't packed.

But he didn't care. "I promise. And you're going to be late." Her voice caught in her throat.

"Screw it," he whispered. "This is the last chance to make love to my beautiful wife before I have to go traipsing across the desert like Lawrence of Arabia." He nibbled at her earlobe while his hand slipped down her belly to the moist heat between her thighs. "Tell you what. You send me a picture of yours and I'll send you a picture of mine. Maybe I can get him a little horse and saddle and send you a picture. Maybe a Barbie camel. I can put him in a little man dress."

She laughed and Carponti's heart swelled in his chest at the sound of it.

"I'm going to hold you to that." She traced her fingers over his scalp, her body soft and warm against his erection. "I want a picture of him in a man dress in exchange for a video of the deployment boyfriend."

Her legs bumped into the back of the bed and he followed her down. Tangled between the duffle bags and his uniforms, he made love to her one last time before he got on a plane and headed to war.

✼ 3 ❊

Early December 2007
Northern Baghdad

Carponti walked up behind his platoon sergeant where he sat on his bunk in the wide- open bay that currently served as their home. Someone had put up a small electric Christmas tree in the corner of the bay. It was supposed to be cheery. Instead, it served as a daily reminder that they were stuck in the desert at Christmas. Carponti had thought about it but hadn't had the heart to take it down. It wasn't like the stupid little tree made a difference to anyone. Least of all his platoon sergeant.

Garrison was stressing the hell out lately and there wasn't much Carponti could do about it. Except try to make his boss laugh. He had an idea he couldn't resist. He fought the urge to laugh as he walked up behind Garrison. "Sarn't G, the XO is looking for you again."

Garrison turned his head and came face to face with Carponti's thumb sticking out of his pants.

"Carponti, what the hell is wrong with you!" Garrison reached across the small space for Carponti's pillow and threw it at him. But he cracked a grin, which was more than he'd done in the last two days.

"Mission accomplished." Carponti removed his hand and buttoned his pants. "What's your problem? You need a hug?"

Garrison sighed heavily, scrubbing his hand over his face. "I'm not in the mood to deal with the XO right now."

"When are you ever? Just go find him before he shows up here and kills all the fun." Garrison lifted one eyebrow and stared at him until Carponti started to squirm. Carponti swore under his breath. Damn it, he needed to get better at lying to Garrison.

"What did you do this time?" Garrison asked.

"Nothing."

"What did you supervise this time?"

Carponti sniffed and his mouth twitched. "Nothing."

"I swear to God, Carponti," Garrison growled. "What did you see happening and not stop?"

"Did you know we have some very talented artists in our platoon?" Carponti couldn't stop himself from laughing because this was the second time someone had defaced the latrine with Lieutenant Randall's ugly mug. "One of the troops drew a new picture of the XO on one of the latrine walls. It's really a work of art. You can completely see the freckles on Randall's nose and everything." Carponti blinked innocently.

"Carponti!"

Carponti pointed over his shoulder. "The XO will be here any minute. I saw him walking into the latrine a few minutes ago."

Garrison laughed quietly, scrubbing his hands over his face. "You're not right in the head." Garrison shook his head and swore beneath his breath. "I really don't want to deal with him today. I'm liable to shove his ego down his throat the next time I see him."

"That would be terrible, just terrible," Carponti said.

"You're not going to go find him, are you?" Garrison said. His leg was bouncing again.

"I mean, if it means that much to you, I'll swing by the company ops and see if I can find out what he wants. But really, we both know I'm just saying that to make you feel better because the almighty executive officer won't deign to talk to a lowly sergeant like me."

Garrison stood and slung his weapon over his chest. "I'll go find him. Just to keep you out of First Sarn't Story's office for screwing with Randall again."

"Taking one for the team," Carponti said, slapping Garrison on the back. "I can't tell you how much that makes me want to write you a Hallmark card." He swiped his finger beneath his eye dramatically.

Garrison flipped him off as he walked out of the bay. Carponti watched him go, wishing there was more he could do to lighten the load. He would have gone to find LT Randall but it wouldn't have done a damn bit of good and everyone knew it. Randall was an epic and unforgettable douche bag and he was making everyone's life miserable.

Especially his platoon sergeant. Garrison liked to pretend everything was fine but Carponti could see the strain of this deployment. Garrison wasn't sleeping well. Hell, no one was. The Surge, as deployments went, sucked. They were getting blown up every time they rolled outside the gate; they were down a half dozen guys who'd gotten hit at various times and well, shit was just ugly.

Carponti was in the not-happy-but-sleeping group of soldiers that included him and...well, him. Everyone was wound too tight, waiting for the next influx of horrible shit to happen and fill up their rucksacks with even more bad news.

Carponti stuffed his hands in his pockets, slung his weapon across his chest, and headed out of the hundred-man bay, where his platoon was stacked up like sardines in a smelly can. The guy in the bunk next to him needed to take a goddamned shower. Carponti was willing to bet that stinky bastard hadn't bathed since the initial invasion back in '03. That was the only way to explain the smell.

Carponti adjusted his weapon and headed toward the company ops. Someone had decorated First Sarn't Story's door with bright red and silver wrapping paper. Story wasn't exactly a jolly type of fellow and he'd sworn something fierce when he'd discovered the defacement. But he'd left it up.

He didn't knock before he entered Trent's office. He walked in to find Trent flipping through a folder, his feet kicked up on his desk. Carponti studied his feet for a moment then decided against saying anything.

Trent looked like he hadn't slept in at least twenty-four hours and possibly more. There was a dirty coffee cup steaming with fresh caffeine near his knee and his hands shook from a combination of too much coffee and not enough sleep. There were dark circles beneath Trent's eyes that his glasses didn't hide.

"You look like shit," Carponti said by way of greeting.

Trent grunted, then a moment later looked up. "Huh?"

"Dude, you need to get some sleep before you pass out."

Trent frowned and tossed the file onto his desk, pushing his glasses up onto his head. "Sorry. Long night. Two more patrols got hit."

"I thought no one got hurt?" Carponti folded his arms over his chest.

"Yeah." He motioned to the wall, a large map of their sector spread across a corkboard. There were pins in clusters surrounding the soccer stadium in their area.

"All the attacks still following the same pattern?" Carponti asked.

"No; that's what's funny. They're decreasing in number," Trent said.

"This isn't exactly a bad thing," Carponti said dryly. "I'm not really a fan of getting shot at."

Trent grinned and took a sip of his coffee. "What brings you by?"

"I'm here to bitch about your executive officer. Why else would I be here?"

Trent's expression shuttered closed. "Randall's not a bad guy."

"He's a raging douche bag and he's not even an effective douche bag. Do you know he was down in the platoon bay demanding we do a weigh-in? We're running patrols every twelve hours and he wants us to do a weigh-in?"

Trent cleared his throat. "Yeah, sorry about that. That decree to conduct the weigh-in has come from on high."

"Are you fucking serious?" Carponti didn't even try to make light of the situation. "The boys are whipped and the powers that be want to do a weigh-in? I think we should be more worried about oh, I don't know, fixing broken weapons and vehicles instead of worrying about whether or not the boys are having too many Twinkies."

Trent held up his hands. "Preaching to the choir. Believe me, I argued and lost. So let's just shut up and color, okay?"

Carponti swore beneath his breath. "Fine." He glanced at his watch. He still had a few minutes before his next hit time.

"Somewhere to be?" Trent asked.

"Calling home. I've got a, um, arrangement with one of the commo kids."

"Is it something I'm better off not knowing about?" Trent asked dryly.

"Probably." Carponti shifted in his chair. "When's the last time you called home?"

Trent frowned. "Not sure."

"You need to be sure," Carponti said quietly. He stood, noticing there was a timeline on the wall behind Trent. He wanted to ask but the shadow that had fallen across Trent's face when he'd brought up calling home worried Carponti. "Speaking of which, I'm late for my own call home."

Trent had more than enough going on but something in his expression made Carponti worry that home was a bigger worry than he let on.

❧

HE CROSSED BEHIND THE TACTICAL OPERATIONS CENTER and pounded on the door of one of the commo shelters. The door swung open slowly, then when the kid inside saw it was Carponti, he opened it all the way.

"Hey, Sarn't C." Jackson was a chubby kid who had an addiction to Oreos and Monster energy drinks. He had a wife who ran around Killeen in a 2006 Escalade, which meant Jackson was always in short supply of cash.

Carponti was not above bribing the kid for a few minutes of alone time with Nicole. Not at all. Carponti slipped him a twenty and Jackson slid it into his pocket.

"You've got thirty minutes until the evening briefing is over. So the network is clear for you."

"You're a great American, Jackson." He patted Jackson on the back as the husky kid climbed out of the shelter.

"Make sure you lock the door, will you? I really don't want to explain to my sergeant why you're whacking it in our shelter."

"Jack, Jack, just 'cause I'm calling my wife and want some privacy doesn't mean..." Jackson shot him a baleful look as Carponti laughed and climbed into the shelter. "I won't leave any evidence."

He closed the door in Jackson's mildly horrified face and flicked the lock into place.

He turned to the terminal and pulled up Skype on the network that had no firewalls to keep him from seeing his wife on the other end.

He waited for her to pick up. Hoped she would pick up. Hoped she wasn't out on an investigation and was actually home. He was damn proud of her that she'd started the new job with the Army's Criminal Investigation Division before he'd left. She was the perfect agent for the job. She looked like someone who belonged on TV instead of investigating the Army's worst of the worst.

But she loved what she did and he wouldn't complain.

He was about to give up hope when she picked up. The screen flickered and darkened and he prayed the network would hold.

Finally, she came into view. Her hair was draped across one shoulder, her eyes sleepy. She'd turned on the bedside lamp so her face was cast in soft light and gentle shadows. God but she was beautiful.

"Damn I miss you," he whispered.

Her smile was sleepy and sexy. "Hi, baby." She leaned up and propped her head up on her palm, slowly waking up. "How are you?"

He swallowed the lump in his throat. He could tell her about the IEDs and the injuries but what was the point? He'd learned on his first deployment that telling her all the bad only made her worry. So he focused on making her smile, on calling enough to make sure she knew he was okay and not rocking in a corner somewhere crying. Sometimes, though, he just wished he could tell her how pointless it all felt.

How he thought about coming home and never leaving again.

But his boys needed him and he hoped, he prayed, that she could continue to understand that. "I'm good. Blowing shit up, just like always. How's the job?"

"I'm good. We're on a new case. I can't tell you too much about it but it's really crazy the things soldiers will do for a very small amount of money."

She was waking up now. Her eyes were bright and he felt like she was actually looking at him now. His heart swelled and a little bit of the bad in his rucksack emptied out, and was replaced with something good from thousands of miles away: his wife's smile.

"Oh, you have no idea. I just paid the commo kid twenty bucks to give me some private time in his shelter while I talk to you."

Nicole grinned, covering her mouth with a yawn. "That's just so wrong."

"But so right." He shifted in the seat, leaning a little closer to the screen, wishing he could crawl into it and end up in their bed. "So I got your last letter."

The first time he'd deployed had been just this side of hell but his wife had figured out how to make it better. He'd been in a big fight in Najaf and had been damn near dead on his feet when the mail had come. And in it had been the first dirty letter she'd ever written him. For a moment, just a few, the war had fallen away as he'd slipped into the fantasy she'd written him. He'd slept like a baby that night and dreamt about his wife and her touch instead of the chaos and smoke of the war.

So it had become a deployment ritual for them. A

way to stay connected through the distance and the silence that often came with deployments.

Her smile warmed. "Yeah? Did you like it?"

"Oh yes. It was inspiring." Carponti shifted to ease the tension in his pants.

I want to feel your lips on my sweet, swollen...

He sucked in a deep breath. His cock stiffened.

"Yeah?" Her hand drifted down her throat, sliding slowly off camera. "Which part did you like the best?"

Carponti cleared his throat, wishing he could see where her fingers went. Wishing they were his instead. "The part where you pulled my underwear off with your teeth."

She laughed but he kept thinking about the hand that had disappeared, wishing he could see where it had gone. The way her chest moved as her breath quickened. "What are you doing?" he whispered.

"Touching myself." Her voice was thick, sultry.

Carponti stopped breathing as all the blood rushed to his cock and it strained against his uniform pants. "Holy crap, warn a guy, will you?"

Her laugh was throaty. Sensual and sleepy mixed together. "Want to know where?"

He cleared his throat again. "Where?"

"Say it," she whispered. "I want to hear you ask me."

"Where are you touching yourself?" He flicked open his uniform pants, freeing his cock, and thanked the powers that be that Jackson kept paper towels and hand sanitizer in his shelter. It wasn't exactly the most romantic setting in the world but he'd take whatever time with his wife he could get. God but he missed her.

He closed his eyes as he fisted his cock, waiting for her answer. "Between my legs. I'm wet. Thinking about you gets me so wet, Vic."

He swallowed, his throat dry as he slid his hand over his erection, wishing it were her hand, her touch.

"Tell me what to do?"

"Slide a finger inside yourself," he whispered when he could remember how to talk.

They didn't get to do this often enough. Hell, he'd do it every night if he could but he didn't like waking her up. Right then, though, with her words wrapping around him, he could almost close his eyes and pretend he was home.

"I want you inside me, Vic." Her voice was a whimper. A plea in the middle of the night that spanned the gulf between them and brought him home, just for a moment. "I want you here."

Her voice broke but she covered it quickly. "I want you here, I want you filling me, deep. Fast." She gasped. "Hard."

"Finish," he whispered, urging his wife to her own climax before he reached his own. "Stroke yourself. Pretend it's my lips sucking on you."

She whimpered again, and her back arched off the bed. She shivered and bit her bottom lip, a smile spreading across her face as she came. He gripped his cock tight as his orgasm ripped through him, tearing out a piece of his heart as he came hard and deep.

"I needed that," she whispered. "I miss you."

"I miss you, too." He licked his top lip, not wanting to get off the computer but knowing she needed to sleep. He smiled at her as he cleaned himself up. "I love it when you do that for me," he said quietly.

She shifted and he could see the swell of her breasts against the tank top she slept in. "It makes me miss you more," she said.

He swallowed, the glow from his orgasm fading as reality crept back in. "I miss you," he said suddenly. He felt the creeping presence of the clock, ticking down, reminding him that he had to go before he got caught. He needed these moments with Nicole more than she knew. "Stay safe at work?"

"I will. I have a new partner and a new case. I've been working out of Waco a lot." Carponti frowned. "What's in Waco?"

"Can't tell you over a nonsecure line but it's an interesting case, that's for sure."

"Be careful? You're not allowed to get shot or anything. I can't promise I won't end up in jail without you in my life."

"It's not like that." She grinned and covered her mouth with her hand as she yawned. "Have you heard anything more about whether you get to come home in a couple weeks?"

Carponti swallowed hard. "I'm trying. Christmas is a hard time to try and get out of theater."

He wished he didn't see the disappointment flicker over her face. "I know you are."

She'd lost her father last year and while her dad had never really liked Carponti, his loss had really done a number on Nicole. Her mom? Her mom was traveling the world and drowning her sorrows in the life of a luxury travel agent to the stars, which meant Nicole would be alone.

Christmas was important to her and Carponti had

missed more than he'd been there for. He needed to be there for her this year. If the damn war would cooperate.

"I'll talk to Garrison about it again. See where I am on the list. I'll e-mail you what I find out."

She smiled and it warmed her eyes. Damn it, he wished he was home, curled around her body. Feeling her breathe. He missed her so badly it hurt.

His watch beeped as the timer went off. "I've got to go."

"Call me again when you can?" she asked.

"I will. I love you," he said.

"I love you. Be safe, okay?"

He grinned. "Of course. And don't think I've forgotten about the video promise. I'm still waiting."

Across the miles, she flushed. "I'm working up the courage."

"Work harder. At this rate, the war will be over before you send me that video. It'll be the highlight of my tour."

She laughed and he wanted to kiss her. He loved making her laugh. God but he missed her. "I'll call soon, okay?"

She nodded. "I love you."

"You, too, babe."

He sat in the silence after the connection died, putting all the happiness from a few moments alone with his wife back in its place, a place the war couldn't touch. He loved her, more than he could ever tell her.

Because when he stepped out of that commo shelter, the war would be back to the top of the list of shit he was focused on.

N icole walked into Target and felt the festive cheer of the holidays. Beside her, Laura scolded her son for running off for the seventeenth time. Ethan—who looked like a miniature Trent—was completely contrite for all of about six seconds before he was lured away by the brightly colored Christmas decorations on yet another end cap. Bright red sales signs advertised Christmas specials and silver tinsel lined the shelves. Of course, it wasn't really Christmas without snow in Nicole's opinion, but they'd lived in Texas for a couple of years now and somehow, she'd gotten used to Christmas in the South.

"I think I'm going to have to adopt this early shopping plan more often," Nicole said. "Even if this is a ridiculous hour to be out of bed on a Saturday morning."

Laura handed Emma a pen and notebook so she could doodle while she sat in the cart's basket. "It's the only way I can manage. All the crowds drive me crazy."

"I can understand that. I can't beat my husband out of the house on payday in Killeen." She pulled out the list of stuff she needed for Vic and tucked her hair behind one ear. This would be the last package she could send him if she wanted him to get it before Christmas. In case he might not get to come home, she still wanted him to have something to open on Christmas. "Does Trent have anything specific he needs?"

Laura sighed. "I wouldn't know because he hasn't called me."

She mumbled the words so that her kids couldn't hear but Nicole didn't miss the worry beneath the bitterness in her voice. She placed her hand on Laura's shoulder. "I'm sure he's just busy," Nicole said quietly.

"When's the last time Vic called you?" Laura said.

"This morning," Nicole admitted.

"And Vic doesn't have a phone on his desk." She blinked rapidly. "I thought I could wait for him to get whatever he's running from out of his system." She bit her lip. "I just don't know how much more I've got in me."

Laura ducked down the office supply aisle and Nicole headed toward the junk food section, giving her friend a moment to collect herself while she gathered junk food and other distractions for Vic. He'd developed a recent addiction to almonds for some reason, so she dropped a couple of tubs of trail mix and mixed nuts into the cart.

For a man who ate like hell, he was an amazing

physical specimen. He never went to the gym but his body was toned and tight from long hours on his feet. Unlike Nicole, who had to hit the gym every day or else.

She turned down the Christmas aisle and bit back a twinge of sadness. God but she hoped he made it home. She wasn't sure she could do Christmas alone. The last couple of times he'd been gone for Christmas, she'd gone home to see her dad. But her dad had left her last year. He'd gotten sick and within four weeks he was gone. His death had stunned her. And Vic? Vic had been her rock during the whole fiasco of sorting her father's affairs, while her mother tried to take everything he had.

She blinked rapidly and felt her phone vibrate in her purse. She dove for it, digging furiously, hoping it was Vic.

It wasn't. It was work. Nicole let it go to voice mail. She wasn't in the mood to talk shop.

Laura found her meandering near the Christmas aisle. Ethan, apparently, had not gotten the message about running off and so was constrained in the shopping cart with a coloring book. Laura looked much happier, despite pushing a heavier cart.

"So, I've got this Christmas party next week for the families and two of my key volunteers decided to go into labor and have babies. I'm shorthanded. Can I please, please, please beg you to help me manage this chaos?"

As a rule, Nicole tried to avoid the Family Readiness Group. It was great for spouses who needed help and guidance and mentorship, but Nicole always felt out of place. Not like she was better than everyone else, but she always felt like she didn't belong when some of the wives would start talking about Pampered Chef or arts and crafts and Nicole couldn't stop thinking about her latest case at work. She wasn't the only spouse who worked but she was the only one in law enforcement.

But this was Laura and she knew Laura was going through her own bad stuff right now with her husband. Nicole had meant to ask Vic if there was anything going on with Trent but she'd forgotten when he'd called. She blamed him for the distraction. She smiled. His call had been a great distraction.

"I guess," Nicole said with a dramatic sigh. "What do you need me to do?"

"Help with the food?"

Nicole arched one eyebrow. "You realize I burn water, right?"

"You can order it. I've got the FRG checkbook." Laura looked relieved and Nicole was glad she could say yes. If only to help her friend.

"So let me buy you coffee and you can talk me through everything you need me to do." Nicole stopped in front of a small Christmas gnome. It had a bushy red beard and bright cheeks. There was a twinkle of mischief in his eyes. Her throat tightened and she swallowed quickly, missing her husband badly.

"Do you know of a coffee shop that has a play area for two small children?"

"No, but that is an amazing idea for some entrepreneurial soul," Nicole said. "McDonalds?"

"Done." Laura sighed. "Thank you so much, hon."

"No problem. Let me finish getting stuff for Vic? I want to get it in the mail this weekend."

"Sure. I've got to pick up a few more things then I'll meet you there."

Nicole nodded as her friend wandered off again in search of the things on her own list. Nicole studied the gnome with the bright red beard.

He was on sale this week. She held him in her hands, wondering what would become of the little fella if she sent him to her husband. She was tempted to keep him here. Put him on the fireplace.

She still had to decorate the house.

Her eyes burned and she breathed deeply to keep the sadness at bay. She wasn't quite ready to do that alone. Not yet. Maybe tomorrow she'd climb into the attic and get the decorations down. She put the little gnome back on the shelf and finished picking up stuff for her husband.

⁂

THE DOOR TO THE FIRST SERGEANT'S OFFICE SLAMMED AS Garrison stepped into the small hallway. Carponti flinched but didn't move from where he stood at parade rest, waiting for the ass chewing of a century.

Lieutenant Randall apparently had no sense of humor.

He dared to glance at Garrison, who stood for a moment in the silence that echoed after the slamming door. "Well, that was fun," he said. "Let's go."

Carponti frowned and glanced back at the first sergeant's festive door. "He doesn't want to see me?"

"Oh he does," Garrison remarked. "But we should really get going before he changes his mind."

Carponti grinned as he followed the big platoon sergeant out of the company ops. "That's a hell of a Jedi mind trick you've got going there. I'm impressed."

"You should be," Garrison said roughly. "He threatened to have you busted all the way back to private."

"He can't prove it was me. I have no artistic talent whatsoever." Carponti grinned. "But you have to admit, the mural on the latrine wall is some really great artwork."

Garrison shot him a long-suffering look. "So great that unless I send the kid who drew it to brigade to work on the t-wall mural, both of our asses are going to be explaining things to the sergeant major."

"I am confident that Tigger will be happy to volunteer his talents to leaving our mark on the Iraqi t-walls." It was tradition that whenever a new unit arrived in theater, they painted their unit crest on a t-wall or jersey barrier.

Garrison sighed heavily. "Look, just stop getting in trouble for a while? We're heading out on patrol and when we get back, I would really like to go to sleep instead of have to bail your ass out of a sling again."

"But you love me so you'll do it," Carponti said.

"I love that you're a fucking machine in combat and I can always count on you," Garrison said. He paused. "And you're damn funny, too."

Carponti sniffed dramatically. "You really should write Hallmark cards."

Garrison grinned. "Shut up and get everyone ready. We're leaving on patrol in two hours and I want everyone's head in the game. Our high value targets are holed up near the soccer stadium. Maybe if we get these guys, we can get some intel on why the attack patterns are dropping."

"The soccer stadium that keeps getting blown up? Lovely." Carponti sobered. "You'd think we wouldn't be complaining about this. Fewer attacks are a good thing, last time I checked."

Garrison shot him a sidelong look as they walked through the maze of jersey barriers back toward the platoon bay. "Normally I'd agree with you but there's such a sharp drop-off that Trent thinks there's another reason. Might be building for a massive attack or something. He's worried about the changing pattern."

Carponti grunted. "He should be worried about calling his wife."

"Yeah." Garrison was quiet for a long moment. "I guess he figures Laura will always wait for him. She's waited this long."

"No woman can wait that long." Carponti drummed his hands on the butt of his rifle. "Hell, I call my wife as much as I can and I'm still worried she'll leave me for her deployment boyfriend. Or worse, a real boyfriend."

Garrison slapped him on the shoulder. "Nicole is the one woman on the planet with a sense of humor enough to match yours. She'll never leave you."

"From your lips to heaven's ears," Carponti said.

He watched Garrison walk off. He hoped that maybe after they got back, Garrison could get some sleep. Carponti buried the niggling worry that taunted him, whispering on the back of his neck. He headed off to start rounding everyone up, wishing he had time to call his wife before they headed out on patrol.

He wanted to hear her voice.

Needed to.

She was his personal good luck charm. As long as she was there in the world, things would be okay.

$\maltese$ 5 $\maltese$

Nicole's phone vibrated next to her bed, dragging her out of her fitful sleep. She blinked and glanced at the alarm clock. Three in the morning. She groped for the phone and saw a mass text message from Laura, sent to everyone on the Family Readiness Group roster.

We have information about an attack. There are injuries but no casualties. Please stay off social networks until we have confirmation of who has been hurt. I will do my best to keep everyone informed.

Nicole sat up, instantly awake, and wiggled the mouse on her computer. Once upon a time, she would have thought it was strange sleeping with a laptop next to her bed, but now? Now it was an easy way for Vic to call her, so she left Skype logged in.

But tonight, her inbox was empty. Nicole swallowed the fear and dialed Laura's number. "Hey," Laura said.

"You don't sound like you've been to sleep."

"I haven't." Laura sounded exhausted.

"How can I help?"

Laura sighed quietly. "You can't. There's nothing we can do right now but wait for more information. And even then, it'll take time for the casualties to be sent from Germany to here. My inbox is going nuts right now."

"That's understandable." Nicole rubbed her eyes. "We're all scared."

"Yeah," Laura admitted. "Me, too."

"Still no word from Trent?" God but Nicole's heart broke for Laura. Her husband was still in silent mode and Laura? Laura's patience was reaching a breaking point. She'd never seen her friend more upset.

"No."

Nicole clicked refresh on her inbox, wishing an e-mail would magically appear and tell her that Vic was okay. She fought the blind panic at his silence.

"I'm sorry," she said to Laura. "I'm so sorry."

Laura said nothing for a moment and Nicole was almost positive her friend was biting back tears. "Me, too. Listen, I've got to get some sleep. Can I call you if I need help?"

"Yeah. Absolutely."

The line went dead and Nicole sat there for a long moment, clicking refresh on her inbox. Just a couple more times. She looked down at the phone and flicked the vibrate off. If Vic called, she wanted to hear it.

She curled up onto her side, staring at the blinking cursor on her computer screen. Her eyes burned, but the fear was too raw, too real. She blinked the tears back, trying her damnedest to keep the ragged fear from breaking free. She stared at the empty inbox as her vision blurred. And clicked refresh again and again as the tears spilled down her cheeks. Just once more before she gave up and tried to go back to sleep.

CARPONTI SAT NEXT TO GARRISON'S BED IN THE OPEN bay of the combat hospital. The hospital was eerily quiet, the silence smothering and oppressive. The chaos and noise and static that had been buzzing around the hospital bed was gone now, leaving nothing but the septic silence. His ribs ached and his chest throbbed but he wasn't in the hospital for his own—comparatively minor—injuries.

They'd gotten blown up. They'd captured their high value target, but the cost? The cost had been really fucking high. The soccer field had been blown all to hell and had taken out Garrison and damn near taken Carponti out, too. His ribs hurt where that rocket had knocked him off the truck. Thank God and Army contractors for body armor that worked. And for guys with shitty bomb-making skills.

There was a tube down Garrison's throat and they were getting ready to move him to the airfield for his flight to Germany. Because the rest of him was pretty banged up. He lowered his head to the bed again. His throat wasn't working right and it was hard to breathe. He blamed his bruised ribs. Couldn't be the raw sadness threatening to overwhelm him. Nope, couldn't be that.

Carponti tried to talk but every time he opened his mouth, his throat closed off again.

There was blood on the floor. They hadn't gotten around to cleaning yet.

The chaos was gone now but for Carponti, the only thing he heard was the steady, rhythmic beep of the heart monitor over the black tattoos on Garrison's chest.

"So listen," Carponti said. "When you wake up —" He cleared his throat roughly. "When you wake up," he tried again. His voice broke but he kept talking because otherwise, he was going to sob like a fucking baby. He scrubbed both hands over his face. He reached for Garrison's hand. The one that hadn't gotten all blown half to hell along with the rest of him. It was warm and listless. Missing the strength and courage of the man Carponti looked up to and wanted to be when he grew up.

"Listen, you're going on a flight. And you're gonna wake up at some point. Be nice to the nurses. 'Cause they're going to take care of your grumpy old ass until you get better. And you need to hurry the hell up and get healthy because you know who they're bringing in to replace you? That asshole Iaconelli from battalion." He dropped his head to his hand where it covered Garrison's. They hadn't waited a day to bring that fucking guy down to the platoon, still reeling from the complex attack that had taken out their fearless platoon sergeant and a couple of the other guys. "So you need to get back here really soon because he's liable to throw my ass out of the Army."

"Sergeant?"

Carponti pinched his eyes before looking up. There was a major wearing scrubs at the end of the bed. She looked like she hadn't slept in about three weeks but there was a sharpness in her eyes. This was a familiar routine for her. Carponti wondered how the hell she—how any of them—kept going when all they had around them were the broken and the bleeding.

She'd done this too many times to be upset by another mangled GI. But Carponti would never get used to it.

Not this.

"We're getting ready to go." She took a step closer and put her hand on Carponti's shoulder.

It took everything he had to keep from shattering from that single, human gesture. He swallowed a couple of times before he could speak. "So you're not going to chop off any body parts while he's unconscious or anything?"

She smiled gently. "We hope not."

Carponti snorted quietly. "That wasn't really a helpful answer." He tried to offer up a smart-ass grin and failed. "He'll be okay, right?" he managed.

"We'll do our best." Her hand squeezed his shoulder gently. "It's time for you to go."

He nodded and stood. He patted Garrison's hand awkwardly. "Don't die, all right, old man? 'Cause there's no telling the amount of trouble I can get into without your old ass keeping me in check."

He walked out then, before his voice broke any more.

Couldn't let the boys see him cry. They had another mission in twelve hours. So he stuffed all the emotion down and bolted it closed.

He'd face that fear and sadness and everything else some other time. Another time when hopefully there would be lots of booze to ease some of the pain.

But for now? Now he stuffed it down and went back to work.

Because that's what Garrison would expect him to do.

❧

"SERGEANT CARPONTI!"

Carponti kept walking, ignoring the voice of that hell-spawned lieutenant. He wasn't in the mood to deal with LT Randall on a good day and today was definitely not a good day.

"Sergeant, I'm talking to you!"

Carponti's temper snapped and he rounded on the XO. "What the fuck do you want, LT?"

"Watch your fucking mouth," Randall snapped.

Carponti sighed dramatically. "You weren't hugged enough as a child, were you?"

"I'm not in the mood for your smart mouth, sergeant."

"And I'm not in the mood for yours."

Randall stepped into his face. "Your buddy Garrison isn't around to protect you now. I'm going to have your ass before this deployment is over."

Carponti smirked. "You can't do anything to my ass. That's a violation of Don't Ask Don't Tell."

"You think you're so funny."

"I know I'm funny. You, on the other hand, have no such redeeming quality." He patted the XO's chest. "What the fuck do you want? I've got a squad of men waiting for information on their platoon sergeant, who just got blown all to shit. Oh, but you wouldn't care about that because you don't know the meaning of the word 'care'."

"I need your paperwork on the sensitive items report."

Carponti swore and stalked off.

"I wasn't done talking to you, sergeant." Randall grabbed his arm.

"I'm done talking to you, LT. Go find my platoon leader for that officer bullshit." Carponti rounded on him, yanking his arm free. "And if you put your hands on me again, I'm going to break your fucking hand."

He stalked off, needing to get away from the XO before he really did something stupid. Because as much as he hated LT Randall, the bastard was right about one thing: Garrison had kept Carponti out of a ton of trouble. If Randall wanted to make an example out of Carponti, now was a prime opportunity.

He really didn't want to call home and tell his wife he'd gotten busted. Maybe he should start watching his mouth.

He grinned bitterly and swiped at his eyes.

Yeah right.

⸙

"Everyone tracking?" Carponti straightened from where he'd been leaning over the sand table and looked around at his boys.

Half of them looked dead on their feet. The other half looked shell-shocked from the attack two days ago. And the one after that. And the one after that. Things hadn't stopped since Garrison had gotten hit. Somehow, they just seemed worse without him.

Their company had endured three more attacks but no more serious injuries. No one was taking things well but in Carponti's platoon, everyone was acting like Garrison had died and he hadn't. There was no way he could take the guys out on the road like this. No one had their head in the game.

Goddamn it.

"All right, look. We had a bad mission but Sarn't G is going to be all right so y'all need to stop moping like a bunch of crybabies." He folded his arms over his chest. "Besides, he's going to be so pissed off when he wakes up. He's got this tube in his dick like, this long." He held his hands shoulder-width apart. "I mean, it's ridiculous."

"How the hell do you know?" Wilks asked.

Carponti forced himself to grin like it was just another day. "Because I drew a smiley face on it before he left."

"Bullshit." This from a skinny kid they called Tigger because he bounced when he played whatever video game they'd stolen from the commo geeks. Tigger was six and a half feet tall and weighed a buck fifty soaking wet but he had some pretty amazing porta pottie artist skills. Not that Carponti was going to tell anyone that. He'd take that shit to his grave before he threw Tigger under the bus for drawing that picture of Randall doing something untoward with a goat.

Carponti placed his palm over his heart. "Hand to God. He's going to get an awesome Christmas present when he wakes up in Germany or the States or wherever they ship his old ass."

Chuckles scattered through the group and Carponti figured it was best not to push his luck. "Everyone rack out. No computers or shit. Just get some fucking sleep. We're going to be busy as hell tomorrow and I don't want Tigger falling asleep in the turret again."

Tigger flipped him off. "One time and I'll never hear the end of it."

Carponti blew him a kiss. "Go to bed, sweetheart. If it gets cold, I'll come snoodle with you."

He waited until everyone was racked out before killing the lights. The hundred-man bay descended into darkness, lit only by the emergency exit lights near the doors and the occasional flashlight as someone ignored the directive to go to sleep. Carponti couldn't summon the energy to care about the few rebels.

"You're not crashing, Sarn't C?" Wilks's bunk was at the foot of Carponti's.

"Nah. I gotta go find LT Miller and the new platoon sergeant and some other shit." Wilks didn't leave. Carponti sat up. "What's wrong?"

Wilks swallowed hard a couple of times. His Adam's apple bobbed in his throat. "Sarn't G's going to be okay, right?"

"Yeah, man. I saw him. He's gonna be fine. Now go the fuck to sleep." The emotions he'd tried to lock down were surfacing, threatening to break free. If the boys saw him fall apart, there was no telling the chaos that would unleash.

So he'd lied. And now he needed to get the hell away from all of them because he was this close to losing his shit completely.

Carponti stalked away from the bay, away from his boys who were all racked out, sleeping off the adrenaline from the constant chaos.

He didn't care where, he didn't know where, he just needed to get away.

Garrison was gone. Jesus Christ, putting Garrison on that MEDEVAC was the most godawful thing he'd ever done.

He slammed back against the nearest barrier, sliding down the concrete. He ground the heels of his hands into his eyes, fighting the grief that ripped through him, tearing and slashing and cutting.

His ass collided with the ground and he pulled his knees to his chest and finally let the grief come, ignoring the pain in his ribs. He wept bitterly for his friend, his mentor, his *brother*. The tears tore out of him, ragged and raw and bitter.

He hadn't been able to get an update on Garrison. Nothing from that fuckwad lieutenant Randall, nothing from the CO. Trent had been more busted up than Carponti at Garrison's condition.

For the first time he could remember, Carponti had no jokes, no smart-ass comments. He'd gotten his boys racked out like Garrison would have expected him to do.

And now this? Garrison would whip his ass if he saw Carponti fall apart like a crybaby in some deserted sector of the base where only the camel spiders congregated. But he couldn't stop. Jesus, he couldn't stop.

He didn't know how long it was before the tears stopped coming. He sat there as the moon slid over the top of the barrier and illuminated the smoke and the dust swirling beneath the stars. Distant explosions echoed in the night.

He should get up.

He should head back. He wanted to call his wife but the words he needed were just...they were gone. He had nothing. No way to tell her what had happened. It was better that she didn't know anyway. She'd worry about him and the last thing she needed to do was worry about him.

He'd call her soon. Whenever he felt like he could bullshit his way through a conversation without telling her everything that had happened. He wanted to call her and just listen to her voice, telling him about something at work or griping about the line at the grocery store. God, he'd give anything to go grocery shopping with her. Something so simple.

He just wanted time with his wife. Just a few minutes alone, listening to her talk. Feeling her breathe on his chest. He'd been gone so much.

He'd call her. Soon. But not today. Because as badly as he needed to hear her voice, she'd hear the sadness in his and she'd worry. He didn't want her to worry. He was terrible at lying to her. Every time he tried to surprise her with flowers or a date night, she caught him.

He dragged his hands over his face. His eyes felt raw and swollen.

He needed to get back. To find LT Miller and check on him. Check on Trent. To *do* something. Anything other than sit there sobbing.

But instead, he sat there, staring up at the stars. He wasn't a praying man. But he sat there, looking at the night sky, unable to think of anything except how tore up Garrison had looked in that hospital bed. A whispered plea crossed his lips.

"Please, let him be okay." His voice broke. His eyes burned.

And after a while, when he was empty and raw, he wiped his eyes, brushed off his pants, and went back to work.

Nicole stepped back and looked at the tree. It tipped slightly at the top but for the most part, it was straight. She reached for her cell phone in the breast pocket of her husband's dress shirt and checked it for the umpteenth time that morning. It wasn't on vibrate. Vic just hadn't called. She slipped the phone back into her pocket and studied the tree.

She didn't think she was going to be able to make it any straighter than it already was. Folding her arms over her chest, she simply stood there for a moment and tried to find the courage to climb into the attic and pull down the decorations.

She sighed hard and reached for the glass of wine she'd poured herself before dragging the tree in off the roof of her husband's truck and into the living room. The scent of fresh pine needles filled the air.

She hadn't gotten a dreaded phone call from Laura, either, which meant that Vic was probably busy, not hurt. She could console herself with that. She didn't really have a choice. The wine was sharp and crisp across her tongue, sliding smooth and easy down her throat.

Her laptop was on the kitchen table. No new e-mails from Vic the last fifteen times she'd checked it. She knew he was okay. But she still wanted to hear it in his voice. Something.

But no matter how many times he'd deployed, she'd never been able to explain to him how hard it was to wait for news. She always worried about sounding like a nag. Like he was over there, dodging roadside bombs and she was bitching at him about a phone call. She knew all she was asking for was a phone call but, sometimes? It felt like she was asking too much.

She took another look at the slightly tippy tree and took another drink of her wine. The silence from her husband made her miss him; that was all. She hadn't had a good laugh in, well, forever.

She padded over to her inbox, looking for the last note from Vic.

Sorry I haven't called much. Been insane over here. I'm fine. We're all fine. Just busy. Will call as soon as I can.

I love you

PS still waiting for that video you promised.

She smiled. The note was from a week ago. She looked at the box on her kitchen table, filled with junk food and five-dollar previously viewed movies.

She could make him a video, right? It wasn't much different from having a glass of wine and writing him a dirty letter.

She swallowed the rest of her wine even as her blood warmed at the thought of touching herself for him. She thought of how surprised he'd be—and how thrilled. She smiled.

She was going to need more to drink.

❦   6   ❦

"**W**hy the fuck aren't your optics tied down to your weapon, soldier?" Carponti looked up as Tigger attempted to stand up straight while the new platoon sergeant, Sergeant First Class Iaconelli ripped him a new asshole.

Carponti tossed down what he was doing and strolled over.

"What's the problem here, Sarn't Ike?" Carponti said, and stepped between him and Tigger. He hated the nickname Ike, which was why Carponti made every effort to call him that.

It must have looked a little strange having a five-foot-ten ginger kid step between two men who were easily six feet tall but, then again, Carponti wasn't exactly counting on having to get into a fight.

But he damn sure wasn't going to sit there and let Iaconelli treat Garrison's boys like they were fucking morons, either.

"Mind your own business, sergeant," Iaconelli snapped.

Carponti tipped his chin. "Tigger is in my squad, ergo this is my business, *sergeant*. So I say again, what seems to be the problem?"

Iaconelli glared down at him and Carponti couldn't miss the fact that his eyes were rimmed with red. Either Iaconelli wasn't a big sleeper or there was something else wrong.

"His optics aren't tied down."

Carponti looked over his shoulder at Tigger's weapon. "They're tied down just fine."

"No they're not. It's not done like this." Iaconelli held up his weapon, which had some intricate mixture of five-fifty cord and hundred mile an hour tape securing his optics to his weapon. "This is how we do it in my old platoon."

"Well," and Carponti turned and held up Tigger's weapon, "this is how we do it in Garrison's platoon."

"This isn't Garrison's platoon anymore," Iaconelli snapped.

Carponti handed Tigger back his weapon. "If you have a new standard, tell us. Don't come in here and get your panties in a twist and start yelling. That's not how we do things here."

Iaconelli looked shocked that a junior ranking sergeant would be so openly defiant but then again, Carponti didn't actually give a shit. Maybe someday his mouth would get him in trouble but right then, with the guys still reeling from losing Garrison, the last thing he was going to let the new guy do was become another LT Randall. Fuck that.

"You'll do things the way I say we'll do things. This is the Army, not a democracy."

Carponti smiled coolly. "Were you potty trained

at gunpoint?" He held open his arms. "Come here, big guy, let me give you a hug."

"If you fucking touch me..." Iaconelli stuck his finger in Carponti's face and Carponti seriously considered planting a kiss on the tip of it. He wondered if Iaconelli would punch him and how much it would hurt. Considering Iaconelli was a fucking giant who spent way too much time in the gym, Carponti would probably lose a couple of teeth before it was all said and done. "Fix the goddamned optics," Iaconelli snapped.

Carponti offered a mock salute. "Yes, master."

"Carponti..." Iaconelli's word was a growled warning. Carponti couldn't have cared less as Iaconelli stomped off.

He turned back to the platoon, who looked somewhere between amused and slightly horrified. "You heard him, ladies. Let's fix the optics so Uncle Ike doesn't have a reason to yell."

Carponti set the guys to work taping down their optics and went back to work on his own project. He wanted to take a few minutes to go see if Jackson would let him call home but lately, the network had been sucking and Jackson had been too busy to let Carponti steal a few minutes.

He hoped Nicole would understand. Goddamn he missed her.

"What are you doing?"

"Oh goody, you're back." Carponti looked up into Iaconelli's face and kept his own expression as innocent as he could. It was an expression Carponti had perfected at the age of six. "I'm sewing; what's it look like?"

"You're sewing?" Iaconelli's hands shook as he folded them across his chest.

"Yep." Carponti could have screwed with him about his hands shaking. He could have asked when was the last time the mean son of a bitch had had a drink.

But he did none of those things. Iaconelli had come on board yesterday, two days after Garrison had gotten sent back to Germany. Carponti had finally gotten the most useless status update ever from Captain Davila: They had no flipping idea how long Garrison was going to be there before he'd get shipped back to the States.

So Iaconelli, the poster boy for interpersonal hostility, was in charge. And to say that Carponti and Iaconelli had differing opinions on things...well, there was a better chance of peace in the Middle East than Iaconelli and Carponti getting along.

He hadn't meant to get into a pissing contest with Iaconelli right off the bat but well, things just kind of happened that way. Until the incident a few minutes ago, Carponti had bitten his tongue because he hadn't felt like being the leader of the insurgency. But he drew a line when someone screwed with his men.

He had other things to worry about. He sat there and sewed the little strip of fabric. It centered him. Reminded him that there was still something good out in the world—his wife.

He hadn't called home in a few days. Every time he thought about it, he felt empty. Cold. He wanted to hear Nicole's voice but he didn't want to talk.

He didn't know what to say. So he said nothing. Maybe he'd still get out of there in time to make it back to Texas for Christmas. He tried to ignore the shadow of Iaconelli standing over him. He wasn't sure he could leave the guys alone with him right now. Carponti didn't trust him and as badly as he needed to be home with Nicole for her first Christmas without her dad, he wasn't sure he could live with himself if something happened to the guys while he was gone.

He couldn't tell her that, though. She'd loved him through choosing the Army so many times, this was the one time she needed him to choose her. He needed to be there for her this Christmas. Less than two weeks away. He could see her soon.

He was holding on to that hope like a lifeline.

"Yes, I'm sewing. Everyone has a hobby. Take Jax over there. He's playing World of Warcraft with a girl in Scandinavia. At least that's what 'she' told him. I suspect it's some bored fat slob on another base somewhere here in Iraq but you can't tell him that. He swears they're getting married."

Iaconelli's face flushed and Carponti could see him trying really hard not to lose his temper. "You're sewing," Iaconelli repeated.

Carponti lifted both eyebrows. "You seem to be hung up on this fact but the simple fact is that yes, I am sewing."

It was almost comical watching the myriad of emotions flash across Iaconelli's face as he tried to find some kind of cogent response. "Have you been to the shrink lately?"

"Clean bill of health after my last explosion."

"Obviously someone missed something if you're sewing," Iaconelli snarled. "Okay, smart-ass, I give up. Why are you sewing?"

"It's for my wife." Carponti grinned in pure innocence. He didn't need to tell Iaconelli what he was sewing. "So she'll send me a dirty video."

Iaconelli's expression twisted into some form of modified horror. For a man who had been on the initial run to Baghdad, that was saying a lot. Carponti smiled and blinked.

Iaconelli held up one hand when Carponti opened his mouth to speak. "Just. Stop."

"What?"

"Not another word. Put the goddamned cross stitch away and get ready to go to a mission brief."

"Do I have time to go call my wife? It's almost Christmas and I want to see if I can get her to talk dirty to me." Iaconelli thought he was kidding. Carponti didn't need to correct him.

He was enjoying Iaconelli's horrified reaction a lot. It had probably been a long time since someone didn't cower at the big platoon sergeant's feet.

Iaconelli started to argue but relented. "I don't give a shit but if I find you whacking off anywhere near my bunk, I'm cutting your dick off."

Carponti smiled. "I love you, too, Sarn't Ike."

"Carponti, I'm not fucking kidding." He looked ready to blow a gasket. Or maybe have a heart attack; Carponti wasn't really sure. Iaconelli choked and turned a slightly different shade of purple. Which was really hard considering his skin was already darker from being in the constant sunshine. It might be almost Christmas but it was still hot as balls and sunny as hell during the day. The nights?

The nights, he froze his ass off. He'd tried to crawl into Iaconelli's bunk the other night— with his sleeping bag—and Iaconelli had threatened to kill him. There was nothing wrong with grown men snuggling to keep warm but apparently Iaconelli would rather freeze than partake of body heat. About five of them had piled into the middle of the bay to keep warm because they hadn't been given enough fuel and well, when the gas ran out, so did the generators that powered the heat in their bay.

So they'd frozen together. And Iaconelli, being the charming SOB that he was, had stayed in his own cot, missing out on a prime bonding moment with his new platoon.

Sarn't Iaconelli had not seen the humor in the situation.

Carponti continued to sew. There was something about the repetition of the needle. He could see why women did this sort of thing. Not that he was going to take up fashion design or anything. He glanced up at Iaconelli. "Did the XO find you?"

Iaconelli sighed heavily. The fact that Lieutenant Jason Randall was a raging asshat was the single point of agreement between the two of them. And neither one of them was about to admit it.

"No. I'm avoiding him. That little fuckweasel can kiss my ass." He zeroed in on Carponti's sewing. "And you need to put that shit away." Carponti could have sworn he heard Iaconelli mutter *It's creeping me out* but that couldn't be right.

Silence hung on between them for a long moment. Carponti didn't like Iaconelli because he wasn't Garrison. Iaconelli didn't like Carponti because he wasn't properly respectful. Carponti thought it wise not to mention that he'd failed basic customs and courtesies in infantry school. Things could be worse.

They could have Randall as the platoon leader. It

was bad enough trying to ignore him as the executive officer. For the life of him, Carponti couldn't figure out why Trent hadn't fired Randall's sorry ass yet, but that was officer business and Carponti tried to stay far, far away from that stuff. So things weren't as bad as they could be. It could be worse but Carponti wasn't in the mood to test the fates.

"Yeah, well, if you don't go find him, then the rest of us are going to have to suffer through him coming in here and honestly? LT Randall smells funny." He looked up at Iaconelli with his best innocent expression. "So would you please go find out what he's complaining about so we don't have to smell him?"

Iaconelli growled and stomped out of the tent, mumbling something about missing his old platoon and whiny little bastards. Carponti grinned and tucked the little stitch of cloth in his pocket and headed across the FOB to the commo shelter and hopefully, a call to his wife, then figured he'd stop by the company ops and check on Trent on his way.

The closer Christmas came, the more depressing the sad little decorations looked. Someone had decorated the counter in the company ops now and there was quiet Christmas music playing as Carponti stepped into the dusty office.

Carponti froze in the doorway.

Lieutenant Randall stood far too close to the only female in the company, PFC Adorno.

Carponti cleared his throat and strolled in, noting the way Randall jumped back. "I thought you worked in the motorpool," he said to Adorno.

She flushed and tucked her cropped dirty blond hair back behind one ear. "I did. I've been pulled up to work in the company."

Carponti frowned, watching Randall attempt to slink away. Oh, wasn't that interesting. Relationships between officers and enlisted were forbidden but Randall was attempting to sleep with one of his direct reports? Interesting, indeed.

He looked at the XO. "Sarn't Iaconelli is looking for you."

Randall sniffed. "He knows where I work."

"God, you are one charming bastard, you know that, LT?"

"Sergeant—"

Trent wasn't in the company so Carponti left before the XO could launch into another diatribe about Carponti's military bearing and disrespect. Couldn't have witnesses around when he told the XO to kiss his ass, now could he?

❧

HE DREADED HER ANSWERING THE PHONE. AS MUCH AS he wanted to hear her voice, a tiny, selfish part of him didn't want her to pick up.

He didn't have the energy to find a way to make her laugh. He was tired. Bone tired. The kind of tired that made him want to sleep for a week. Maybe then things would be okay.

Maybe then he'd find his missing sense of humor.

"Hey." Her voice slid over his skin, a balm over all the ragged exposed wounds.

"You awake?"

Nicole's voice was tired. "I'm working."

"Oh yeah?"

"Yeah." Her smile was soft and sexy. "It's that

case I can't really tell you much about. I'm with my partner and we're on the way back from Waco."

"He's keeping his hands to himself, right? I don't have to come home and like, unleash my PTSD on him, do I?"

She laughed quietly. "No, honey. David isn't going to violate your precious."

He smiled, wishing they were alone so he could tell her how much he missed her. But they weren't. So small talk it was. "So did you decorate the house for Christmas yet?"

"I started but...it's hard without you. Have you heard anything else about R&R? Are you still trying to get home?"

He swallowed the lump in his throat. "I'm on the list for next week. If the fates align, the planets are all in conjunction and Sarn't Ike doesn't get his period, it'll work out." He paused, unable to tell her that he was thinking about pulling his leave until things settled down. It felt wrong to think about leaving his platoon over the holidays. But instead he said, "I really want to be there for you. I know this Christmas is going to be hard."

"Yeah." A rustle of fabric. "I want you home, honey."

"I know. Trust me, I'm having a blast on my vacation over here in the desert. It's so much fun getting blown up every day."

"Not funny." She sniffed. "Is it that bad?"

He shrugged, even though she couldn't see it, and leaned forward, cupping his face in his hands. "It's not that bad. It could be worse."

"How?"

"We could be getting attacked multiple times a day."

"Not funny."

He smiled. "It's a little funny."

"No, it's not." She was serious. Shit. He hadn't actually meant to freak her out.

"Hey, so I made something for you."

"Made something? What, do you have arts and crafts hour between patrols?" The laughter was back in her voice but there was an edge. Something sharp and wary. A barrier he didn't want between them but a barrier he couldn't scale nonetheless. Not then. Not at all.

Because his rucksack was just too full of bad news for him to force any sarcasm through.

"Yeah. I'll give you two guesses."

"I have absolutely no idea."

"Really? Think back to the night I left."

She sighed and he heard the exasperation in her voice. Shit, he wasn't usually this inept with her. "Man dress."

She laughed. But it wasn't the same. Probably because dickwad David was in the car. He shouldn't hate the man but Carponti was tired and feeling slightly peevish. David could have been Mother Teresa's great nephew twice removed but at that moment, he was taking time from Carponti and his wife.

He rubbed his thumb between his eyes, needing to tell her all the bad shit. Wishing he could unload some of it and she could tell him something good to replace the bad.

Maybe he should have told her about Garrison but if she knew he was hurt, she'd worry. And she needed to focus on her job right now, not worry about what her husband was going through downrange.

So he kept quiet and the silence grew on the line. Finally, his patience snapped. "Look, I know you can't talk much right now. I'll try to call again soon?"

"Yeah. Hon?"

"Yeah?" He frowned and waited, his breath catching in his throat.

"I really hope you make it home for Christmas."

He swallowed. "Yeah, me, too."

He disconnected the call before he let his temper get the better of him and walked out of the shelter and back toward his bay. Nicole didn't deserve him being a douche bag at the moment but he'd really hoped she'd laugh at the man dress costume.

And when she didn't...okay, she had but not like she would have if she'd been alone.

He dropped the little piece of fabric on his bunk as he grabbed his kit and headed toward the mission brief, trying to smother his disappointment. His one skill in life was making his wife laugh and tonight he'd fallen flat on his face. He tried not to let it bother him. He wanted to brush it off.

He failed. The one thing he'd needed, badly, was to hear her laugh. To replace some of the miserable strain of the goddamned war with something good and pure.

He barely listened as Iaconelli briefed the plan, his thoughts a thousand miles away, missing his wife.

NICOLE STARED AT HER CELL PHONE IN THE DIM LIGHTS

inside the car and fought the urge to cry. The whole conversation was stunted and…off. Fear curled up inside her heart. Something was wrong. Vic was never serious unless something was wrong.

She flipped the phone in her hands, unable to put the emotions churning inside her back in the box. God but she didn't want to cry. Not at work.

"You okay?" David's gentle voice broke the silence. He was older than she was by at least fifteen years.

"Not really," she said, hoping her voice wouldn't break.

"Deployments are tough duty." He drummed his fingers on the dashboard, the movement creating little shadows in the interior lights. "I'm sorry you're having a hard time."

"I'm worried about my husband," she whispered. "He's scaring me."

"I deployed on the initial invasion into Iraq," David said after a while. "Desert Storm, not the Thunder Run. The news made it sound like we sliced through the center of Iraq and woke up in Baghdad. It really wasn't that easy." He paused. "It was the first time my wife and I had ever been apart. She wanted me to call home every chance I got."

Nicole looked at him. His weathered face was cased in shadows, his dark skin lined with experience. "Did you?"

He shook his head. "No. I couldn't. There was stuff I couldn't talk to her about. There's still stuff I don't bring up. And it's hard because she wants to know what the war was like. I can't talk about all of it." He glanced at her quickly. "Going to war isn't all

PTSD and trauma. It's just some stuff is hard to talk about."

"How did you make it through?" Nicole asked quietly. His words had struck home. She did want to know. She hated not knowing. It hurt her, knowing that Vic wouldn't talk to her but David's words sank in. Maybe he *couldn't* talk right now.

"I talk to her when I can. Try to share some things with her. But mostly, she listened when I told her there was some stuff I just couldn't talk about and I asked her to be patient with me."

"Is she?" She admired David. He was a mentor and a friend. It was difficult to picture him as less than a perfect gentleman.

"She gets frustrated with me. I shut down some-times. But yeah, she's there for me." He reached forward and turned down the air conditioner. "I don't know what would have happened to me if she hadn't stuck with me. Even when I was drinking myself stupid every night."

"You drink?" This was new information.

"I quit. Wrapped my car around a tree about six years ago. CID stood by me and supported me while I went through treatment. So did my wife." He pulled up in front of her house. The outside light shined like a beacon in the darkness. "So I can't tell you what to do but if you still love him, hold on until he gets home. Give him some time to process everything."

Nicole swallowed the sadness blocking her throat and nodded. "Thanks, David."

"For what it's worth, I'm sorry you're going through this."

She closed the door quietly behind her. It was

reassuring that he didn't pull off until she closed her front door and clicked off the outside light. The Christmas tree stood in the corner, a dark unlit shadow. She hadn't managed to get the lights on it yet. Every time she started, she just got too sad.

She turned her phone off vibrate and plugged it in next to the bed. Then she turned on the computer and logged in to Skype, hoping, praying that her husband would call her back.

She slipped out of her clothes and into one of Vic's shirts. She tried not to cry as she sprayed his cologne on her wrists, needing the familiarity of his scent even if she was missing the warmth of his body in the bed next to her.

But when she slipped between the sheets and pulled a pillow to her belly, she let the tears come. Great, wracking silent sobs broke through and she cried until she couldn't stop.

"I just want him home."

But it was a plea to the darkness that no one heard.

7

Iaconelli's hands weren't shaking. Carponti watched his new platoon sergeant as he talked with their platoon leader LT Miller just to be sure. Nope, no shaking.

Which meant one of two things: either Iaconelli's DTs had finally eased back or he'd gotten his hands on some alcohol.

Carponti wasn't a betting man but he was willing to bet Iaconelli had found some booze. Any and all sins were available in Iraq; you just had to know where to look and be willing to pay for them. He supposed it was just like America after all.

Carponti took a pull off his Dr. Pepper and debated his actions. It had been less than a week since Garrison had gotten sent home and Iaconelli was no more integrated into the platoon than he'd been at the start of this little adventure.

It didn't help that two more guys were getting stitched up at the aid station. But they were coming back with a prescription for Motrin and a good night's sleep. Carponti couldn't blame Iaconelli directly for them getting hurt but that didn't mean he wasn't going to try. He couldn't keep drinking on the patrols. He didn't care how much of a functioning alcoholic the man was; his drinking was going to get someone killed.

It could have been worse. He kept reminding himself of that. He reached his hand into his pocket and felt the little piece of fabric that made up the man dress.

It had been funny when he'd started on it a few months ago. He'd sat on his cot and thought about taking pictures and sending them to his wife. Now, after that last phone call, he started to think it was just stupid. He'd wanted to call her back but every time he'd tried to break away, something had come up.

He felt like an asshole leaving the last conversation like he had. It wasn't her fault she'd been working that night. Carponti had been a shit and he knew it. He wanted badly to call her back, damn it.

But if he was honest with himself, and he really didn't make much of a habit of telling himself lies, he was terrified to pick up that phone. He was afraid she wouldn't answer. That maybe the distance on the line hadn't been his imagination.

That maybe, this time, she'd finally gotten tired of waiting for him to come home.

Things were weird between them this deployment. He knew it was him not calling as much. Putting space between them. He didn't have it in him to pick up the phone and listen to her talk about work. He used to love hearing her talk about nothing at all. Now? Now he just couldn't summon the energy to care. He was too tired. Too worn down. The war was kicking his ass and he didn't know how to be normal on the phone with her. Maybe that made him a prick but the war—the war was taking everything he had right then.

He hoped she'd understand. Maybe he'd get to go home next week after all.

The thought of getting on a plane and leaving his boys, though... He wasn't sure he could do it. He knew the commander would let him stay if he told him he wanted to push back the R&R dates. Captain Davila wouldn't argue, especially not since he'd just lost Garrison as one of his key leaders.

"Sarn't Carponti!"

Carponti stuffed the fabric back into his pocket and pasted on a bored expression as he turned. "Yes, your highness?"

LT Randall's skin tightened over his bones as he kept coming and stepped right into Carponti's personal space. "You will call me fucking 'sir', you arrogant little bastard."

Carponti didn't really think about what happened next. He blinked and the next thing he knew, strong hands were dragging him off the LT. Iaconelli's big hand shoved him backward. "Cut the shit, Carponti," Iaconelli growled.

But Carponti wasn't done. He squared off with the lieutenant, ignoring Iaconelli's attempt to pull him off. "Don't fucking talk to me like that, you scumbag motherfucker."

"Goddamn it, Carponti!"

They were nose to nose. Randall's face was swollen, just like his fucking ego, but there was triumph in his eyes. "You just crossed the line. I'm going to have your rank for this, Carponti," Randall snapped.

"Good luck with that," Carponti spat.

"That's not how this works, *Sergeant*." Randall spat the word. "You will respect my rank."

Carponti shoved Randall a step backward. "That's exactly how it's going to work. Stop harassing my guys because of your incompetence, lieutenant. You lost the fucking equipment, you find it. But leave my goddamned men alone."

The veins in Randall's neck stood out against his skin. Carponti was reasonably certain the man was going to have a coronary.

It would have been one memorial ceremony he'd have been happy to attend.

Iaconelli finally moved his hand off Carponti's chest and stepped into the fray, shoving Carponti back and stepping between them. "LT, what's missing?" he asked.

Carponti frowned as one of the guys came up to watch the fireworks. It was Neal Sloban, a guy who'd been with Carponti since the middle of the last rotation.

"Since when did Iaconelli become a voice of reason?" Sloban muttered.

Carponti shrugged. "I have no idea. Maybe his horoscope told him to play nice today."

Sloban shook his head and walked off as Carponti continued to watch the de-escalation between the two, like Iaconelli was some kind of lieutenant whisperer. Randall finished gesticulating wildly and stomped off. Iaconelli hesitated a moment before he walked back toward Carponti.

"That was impressive," Carponti said as Iaconelli walked back to the waiting convoy.

"I have my specialties."

"You have to tell me how you did that." It was a strange truce between them. Half the time, Carponti was certain that Iaconelli was going to whip his ass if Carponti made one more smart-ass comment. Which of course, Carponti did. Iaconelli never laughed, though.

"I threatened to knock his front teeth out if he didn't stop fucking with my platoon."

Carponti laughed and stuffed his hands in his pockets. The piece of fabric made him think of his wife. Something slipped out, something briefly happy in the midst of the fucking sadness that had been haunting him since he'd watched them put Garrison on the plane.

He needed to call home. Right then, before they rolled out the gate. He glanced toward the company ops.

He didn't have time. Damn it, he didn't have time.

He brushed his thumb over the fabric in his pocket. He'd call her when he got back to the FOB.

He swallowed and pulled his helmet on. He'd finish sewing when he got back to the base.

It would have to be good enough. He'd been an ass and he really needed to hear her tell him that she still loved him.

۞

CARPONTI DUCKED BEHIND THE TIRE OF THE TRUCK THAT was currently the only thing providing even a smidgen of cover for the last half of their convoy. Rounds exploded overhead even as Tigger manned the fifty cal and tried to lay down suppressive fire.

Their convoy had gotten hit exactly one block outside the base. Carponti would be pissed off later. Right then, he needed to get his boys set on the defense and figure out if anyone was wounded back in Sarn't Iaconelli's truck.

Iaconelli, in the trail vehicle, had been hit by the IED that had blown the front end of his truck all to shit.

Carponti ducked and rushed from his own vehicle to where Iaconelli was leaning on Carponti's seat, blood running down the side of his leg and talking on the radio. "Sarn't Ike, you realize you've got blood pouring out of your ass?"

"Shut the fuck up, Carponti. I'm trying to call this in." He paused, his face going grey for a brief moment. "Where's the LT?"

Carponti glanced toward the front of their patrol, where he saw Miller directing some of the guys. "He's getting the lead vehicle out of the kill zone."

"Security?"

"Security is set. I've got Foster and Sloban manning the rear position. LT is going to recover the downed vehicle or blow it in place, then we're going to get the hell out of here."

Iaconelli was leaning against Carponti's truck, the hand mic from Carponti's radio in his hand. "Casualties?"

"None, other than your ass, apparently."

Iaconelli looked like he wanted to punch him. A piece of concrete blew off the building and Carponti ducked. It bounced off his eye pro and he jerked his head, cracking his helmet on the side of the vehicle.

"You're going to want to apply pressure to that," Carponti said when his vision had cleared up. He reached for Iaconelli's first aid kit.

Iaconelli slapped his hand away as he listened to the radio. "Not in this lifetime."

Carponti stood there for a second, completely speechless. Then he started laughing.

"Then you need to let the medics check you out, because that's a shitload of blood and you're so pale you look like the Emperor on *Star Wars* right now, which, for a brown guy, is pretty fucking pale."

Iaconelli shot him a dirty look. "Are you ever serious?"

"I try not to be. Bad things happen when I'm not making jokes. It upsets the cosmic order of the universe or something." He glanced around at Iaconelli's bloody uniform. "Still bleeding. And the sergeant major is calling you."

Iaconelli sighed heavily and lifted the hand mic to his face so Carponti could get the bandage from his first aid kit. Carponti grinned as he pulled the bloody uniform away from Iaconelli's ass. "You have such firm, round..."

"Carponti, I swear to Christ—" He broke off listening to the radio.

"What? I was giving you a compliment." He pulled the fabric away from Iaconelli's ass, tearing the rest of his uniform all to hell. "Well, it could be worse," Carponti mumbled.

"Stop the goddamned bleeding and get the hell away from my ass," Iaconelli growled. "Roger that. Reaper Main. Two vehicles."

Carponti focused on the task at hand, which started with cutting a bigger hole in Iaconelli's trousers. He pulled the end off his Camelbak and flooded the wound with water so he could see what he was dealing with.

"Oh, you're not going to like this," he said.

There was a piece of metal sticking out of Iaconelli's buttock. A small one the size of a penny, but still. It was a sharp penny.

"What?" Iaconelli twisted to look over his shoulder.

"Are there any arteries in the ass cheek?" Carponti asked.

"You're kidding, right?"

"Nope. 'Cause I can put this dressing on your wound but, well, I'm thinking it's going to hurt worse than if we wait for the medics to pull this thing out of your ass." He beamed as Iaconelli glared at him. "I've always wanted to use that phrase in a sentence."

Iaconelli turned purple. Yes, definitely purple. "Just...just use your Leatherman or something and take care of business."

"This is going to hurt." Carponti chuckled and pulled his Leatherman out. "One. Two. Two and a half..."

"Just fucking do it," Iaconelli snapped.

But Carponti had been counting on irritating Iaconelli with the countdown. The minute he'd snapped, Carponti had seized the shrapnel and tugged.

Iaconelli hissed and swore between gritted teeth. The shrapnel popped free. Blood flowed freely but he got the pressure dressing in place. Kind of. "There's really no good way to tape something to your ass this way," he muttered, more to himself than to Iaconelli. He started cutting strips off Iaconelli's tattered uniform to tie the bandage in place. "It's going to take more than a Band-Aid."

He leaned around Iaconelli. "You want to save this?" He held the piece of metal in the tongs of his pliers.

Iaconelli grunted and waved Carponti off. He plunked the metal into Iaconelli's pocket. He'd want that later. Maybe. If not, he could sell it on eBay or something.

❧

You've reached Nicole Carponti. Leave me a message and I'll call you back.

Carponti's heart sank in his chest as her voice mail beeped. "Hey, baby, it's me. Just got back from taking a piece of metal out of my platoon sergeant's ass. I think this means we're BFFs now." He sighed and rubbed his eyes. "Sorry I missed you. I'll call again soon."

He hung up, breathing deeply to push aside the disappointment in his chest. He walked away from the call center, back toward the open bay where he and the guys were bunking, and figured he'd try to get some sleep.

Hopefully, he wouldn't get blown up in the middle of his nap. That would suck. One of the life support areas had got hit last week. Luckily, the guy who'd lived in that trailer had been banging the division commander's aide de camp across the base at the time so he hadn't been home.

It was nice to just sweep a bunch of shit into the trash instead of having to attend another ramp ceremony saluting a flag-draped coffin on its final flight. God but he hated those ceremonies. He swallowed and stepped into the bay.

There was mail on his cot. From a few feet away, he could see his wife's neat handwriting on a small package.

He suddenly couldn't breathe. He sat down, back to the rest of the bay. Iaconelli had taken over Garrison's cot but he wasn't there right now. He was busy getting his ass stitched back together. It was as close to privacy as Carponti could get without asking Jackson to use his commo shelter, and Jackson was on a mission down at Camp Victory or something so he wasn't about to go ask one of the other kids.

His hand shook like a schoolgirl's as he sliced the top off and pulled out the letter and...

And a CD. In neat block letters was the word *private*.

He opened the letter.

I swear to God if the rest of your platoon sees this, I'll divorce you.

He could almost hear her scolding him with a smile on her face. Every emotion he'd locked down came tumbling out and he blinked hard and quick against the wetness in his eyes. He'd guard that CD with his life.

Okay, now that we've got that clarified, I made you a Christmas present in case you can't come home. Well, two presents (read the next page). I really want you home, Vic.

I miss you. I'm not going to moan on and on (next page) but I just need to tell you that. I love you, more than anything else. So I don't care what you have to do, just come home to me, okay? Because I'm going to be really upset if you die. Just so you know. Now go someplace private and read the next page. I love you.

Nicole

Carponti sat for a long moment, just reading her letter again and again. The sound of her voice in his head was as clear as if he was on the phone with her.

He wasn't sure if he dared to read the letter. It wouldn't be cool if he started walking around with a raging hard-on in the middle of a bay full of dudes. Then again, it would probably piss Iaconelli off to no end. He laughed. He should leave a crumpled up, wet paper towel on Iaconelli's cot just to screw with him.

It would be funny to watch him freak the hell out.

'Course, he might actually knock Carponti's teeth out. That would certainly put a damper on things. Go home after the war and talk to his wife like the Gopher on Winnie the Pooh.

Carponti read his wife's letter once more, then slowly turned to the next page.

I miss you. I lay awake at night, thinking about you. I miss the little things. The sound of you getting up at night. The feel of your body in bed with me. I sleep in the middle of the bed when you're gone.

Sometimes, I can almost pretend you're here with me. I wear your cologne to bed and close my eyes. My nipples tighten. I imagine it's your fingers teasing them.

Your tongue tasting them.

I miss the way your mouth feels on my body. The way your fingers could slide between my thighs and make me wet. My fingers slide down my stomach. My nipples brush against the cool sheets. I'm wet for you, Vic. I can feel your fingers stroking my pussy. I want you to fill me. To touch me the way only you know how.

My back arches as you fill me. Make love to me, Vic. I miss you so much. I miss the way you move inside me. I'm wet, so wet. I want you. Faster. Inside me. Harder. I want to feel you all around me. My breath catches as I come around you, vibrating, shaking, surrendering to your touch.

I love you.

Carponti was going to embarrass himself if he stood up. It was going to be damn near impossible for him to stand up, let alone make it to the latrines a quarter mile away without anyone seeing his erection. He pulled his pillow over his lap and just sat there, reading her words again, hearing her voice in his head.

He smiled and couldn't care less. His wife loved him enough to violate several federal laws and a couple of general orders, and send him a dirty letter and better yet, a dirty video.

He curled into his bunk and onto his side. For a brief moment, he shut out the world and thought about his wife. For a moment, he forgot about the shit war in the shithole country and all the bad things that had been happening recently.

He closed his eyes, and let his mind drift back to the States. To the beautiful sexy woman waiting for him.

❧

NICOLE STEPPED OUT OF THE SHOWER AND WRAPPED HER body in a towel. She was exhausted after pulling thirty-six hours of duty. She'd barely managed to stay awake long enough to shower but the entire time she'd been in there, she'd been listening for the sound of her phone.

She padded through their bedroom toward her phone.

Missed call.

Damn it, damn it, damn it.

The voice mail notice vibrated in her hand. Tears welled in her eyes as she listened to Vic's message.

He sounded terrible. Her heart cracked in her chest and she sat down on their bed, giving into the exhaustion and the sadness. She was so tired of the war.

She curled into a tight ball and wept bitterly. Vic's voice was so off. So tired. He was avoiding her. He always did that when bad things happened. She knew it but she still didn't like it.

She'd prayed he'd call, that she'd get to hear his voice. But she heard his voice. And it wasn't enough. Damn it, it wasn't enough.

She listened to his voice mail again, cursing herself for forgetting to turn the vibrate off.

She pushed up off the bed and wiped her eyes, then went back into the bathroom. She found his cologne and sprayed it on her wrists and chest. A lonely ritual but one that kept her sane.

Then she pulled on a pair of his old sweatpants and climbed onto his side of the bed, hugging a pillow close and breathing in his scent, and trying to ignore the breaking of her heart in her chest.

8

"Hey, Carponti."

Carponti frowned. He'd been having an amazing dream about his wife, her deployment boyfriend and a bottle of lotion. He really didn't want it to end but damn it, someone was poking him in the back.

"Unless you're checking my kidneys, stop touching me," Carponti mumbled.

"Wake up, man. You gotta hear this." It was Tigger.

Carponti groaned and sat up. "What the hell is so important you had to wake me up?"

"We're on lockdown."

Carponti frowned, scrubbing his hand over his face. "Why?"

"There's a bunch of shit going down about some missing optics."

Something sank in the vicinity of Carponti's heart. Missing optics were on par with missing weapons systems. As in, really not good. "What missing optics?"

Tigger shrugged. "I don't know but everyone's talking about it. Randall's apparently got to go get sworn statements from some of the guys back in the States. And there're rumors that the commander is going to get fired."

"Why the hell does the LT need to go back to the States to get statements?"

"It's what everyone's saying. I figured you knew."

Carponti shook his head. "No, I haven't heard anything. And for the record, news about that fuck-tard Lieutenant Randall was not important enough to wake me up from dreaming about my wife."

Tigger stood, looking completely unfazed. "Yeah, well, something's going on. You might want to find the platoon sergeant and see what's up. I think we're on lockdown until the commander figures this stuff out."

Carponti swore and dragged on his uniform. "I'll go see what's going on," he said. He was still irri-tated that he'd been woken up for some drama at the company but he'd lied when he'd told Tigger it wasn't important enough to wake him up.

Missing optics was definitely on the list of things to wake someone up for.

He crossed the base quickly, walking into the company ops. Since the new soldier had started working up there, the ops had gotten decorated with more and more Christmas stuff. Someone needed to give the ops clerks more to work on before it exploded with Christmas cheer.

He walked into the commander's office without

knocking. Trent was busy typing away and motioned for Carponti to sit while he finished whatever he'd been working on.

"So what's this I hear about you firing the XO?" Carponti asked.

"Sadly, I'm not firing him." He tossed his glasses on the desk. "I don't have any cause to fire him."

"Missing equipment seems like it might be a good reason," Carponti said.

"Yeah, well, he's investigating said missing equipment, not the cause of it."

"Sure. Whatever you say."

Trent frowned. "What's that supposed to mean?"

Carponti looked around the office, searching for the words he needed. "I'm just thinking that Randall's got some integrity issues, that's all."

"Anything you can prove?" Trent asked cautiously.

"Nothing other than supposition and rumor," Carponti said. "But is he really being sent home?"

"If he can't find the stuff here, yeah." Trent grinned humorlessly. "And on top of all of that, I have to report to the commander that we've done a hundred percent weigh-in. So are you ready to go get a class on how to properly evaluate body fat?"

"You're serious?"

"Yep. We've got professional development class in..." He glanced at his watch. "Five minutes. I get to be the guinea pig for first sergeant to demonstrate the proper conduct of the Army's body fat test."

Carponti sighed dramatically. "I'm quite confident I have never been to war before when garrison broke out. You realize this is stupid, right?"

Trent stood, circling the desk. He slapped Carponti on the shoulder. "Oh yes. Very much so."

⚜

Nicole stood in the lounge at her office headquarters and scanned the news ticker for any information about her husband's base. She flicked the vibrate button on her cell phone. On and off. On. Off.

"Hey, Nicole, we're going out for drinks to celebrate. Are you...?" Major Olivia Hale stuck her head in the door then paused and came all the way into the break area. "Are you okay?"

Nicole offered a smile and hoped it passed for a reasonable facsimile. "I'm fine. Just waiting for news, that's all."

"Yeah, it's been a bad week for attacks across the board." Olivia glanced at the TV. "I'm sure your husband is fine," she said quietly.

"I know. I just, I worry, that's all."

Olivia sighed and tucked her hands into her pockets. "A few of us are going out to drink to celebrate putting that sex offender in jail. Want to join us?"

Nicole glanced down at her cell phone. Somehow, it felt wrong going out to the bar while her husband was deployed, suffering through God only knew what. She shook her head slowly. "I'll pass, thanks. I've got some last minute Christmas stuff to do."

"Christmas isn't for another ten days. You obviously don't know the meaning of the phrase 'last minute'," Olivia said dryly.

Nicole looked down at her phone.

"Ah shit, honey, I'm sorry," Olivia said quietly.

Nicole covered her mouth with her hand and tried to keep the tears at bay. "I'm okay," she said finally. "I'm gonna go." She offered an apologetic hug. "Sorry. This Christmas is just really hard."

She left before Olivia could talk her into staying. She felt out of place and off kilter since she'd missed Vic's call, and as Christmas cheer spread, her mood only sank further into unhappiness.

She tried to tell herself he'd be home if he could. That he'd call if he could. That everything was fine; it was just the war.

She thought about going home but instead detoured to Laura's office. She wasn't sure she wanted to be alone right now. Maybe she should have just gone out with everyone from work but she was confident she'd have just been alone in the crowd of celebratory cheer.

She knocked on Laura's office door a few minutes later. Her friend looked up from her computer and Nicole was rocked by how upset and tired her friend looked. "I was coming to see you for moral support but it looks like you might need it more than I do," Nicole said quietly.

Laura swallowed and said nothing for a long moment. Then she handed Nicole a plain manila folder.

Nicole read the first page before she nearly dropped it like she'd been burned.

Laura Davila, Plaintiff—

"You can't be serious, honey," Nicole said.

Laura was trying hard not to cry but her eyes rimmed with red anyway. "He's breaking my heart," she whispered. Her voice broke.

Nicole closed the door behind her then walked

around the desk, pulling her longtime friend into a tight hug.

God damn the war that did this to them.

To all of them.

"I haven't heard from him in weeks. Weeks. I'm the Family Readiness Group leader and I don't know what's going on. I can't tell any of the spouses that. We've got attacks daily and I don't know if he's hurt or if anyone else is." She pulled out of Nicole's embrace. "But the worst part is the emptiness. I can't keep crying myself to sleep over him. It's been years." She swiped at her eyes. "I keep waiting for him to come home from the war." She sighed quietly. "I don't think that day is going to come," she whispered.

Nicole looked down at the divorce papers on Laura's desk. "You can't... Just wait. Give him more time. There's got to be a good reason."

"You know what the rumors are? They say he's cheating on me." She smiled pitilessly. "But the worst? The worst fucking thing I've heard? He's been volunteering. Every single deployment he's been on, he's volunteered for." She pressed her lips together. "I can't keep having faith in a man who gives me no reason to believe in him," she whispered.

Nicole pulled her close again, offering nothing more than silent support. If she was going to do this, Nicole would support her.

But fear was a powerful thing and it slithered beneath her skin, whispering that nothing and no one was safe from the strain of war.

"No, you can't use my camera."

"Come on, Tigger, please?" They had a mission in less than six hours. Carponti needed a damn camera and the world was conspiring against him.

"No."

"I'll pay you." Carponti couldn't find his camera. He was convinced that LT Randall had stolen it but he couldn't prove it and so he kept the allegation to himself. That sneaky bastard had been caught with one of the soldiers' iPods a few months ago and had denied stealing it.

The commander had told him to give it back and let the matter drop. But that didn't make anyone any more trusting of the LT. Randall was the epitome of a toxic leader, the Army's favorite new buzz word. He practically came with a biohazard warning.

He'd finished the man dress he'd been sewing and now he wanted to send the picture home to his wife. He'd woken up that morning with a feeling of sick dread tying his guts in knots. Sending the pic home to his wife was suddenly the most pressing task he needed to accomplish.

Ever since Garrison had gotten hurt, Carponti hadn't felt right. He knew it was grief and all that other shit the counselors liked to say, but this felt different. He *had* to send that picture home to his wife. Something was hanging over his head that if he didn't get that picture sent home, something bad was going to happen.

He hated when he got those feelings because, damn it, something bad always happened. And he *hated* being right about crap like this.

They were heading out on a mission later tonight

and damn it, Carponti wanted that picture in Nicole's inbox when she woke up.

At least that way, if he died, she'd always have a picture of a little outfit he'd made with love to keep with her instead of whatever was left of him that they sent home.

And wasn't that a depressing thought. It was enough to make him need a hug. He glanced toward Iaconelli, busy cleaning his weapon. He doubted Iaconelli was the hugging type.

Shit, he was feeling melancholy.

He tried again to get Tigger to let him borrow his camera. "I'll sanitize it before I bring it back."

"I said fucking no," Tigger snapped and rolled over in his cot.

"You could have just said so," Carponti grumbled.

Damn it. He stalked out of the bay and headed to the company ops. Maybe he could convince Trent to let him borrow the company camera.

'Course, he'd have to figure out how to delete the picture. Or maybe he'd leave it on there. Oh, to be a fly on the wall when the ops sergeant used the camera next time. That would be awesome.

Carponti grinned as he pushed through the plywood and two by four contraption that constituted the door to the company ops.

"Roger that, sir. I understand."

Carponti frowned and stopped by the door, not sure who Trent was talking to. Whatever it was, it didn't sound good.

"Roger, sir." Trent looked up then motioned for Carponti to come all the way in.

"Roger."

Trent hung up the phone and looked at it for a long moment, then, as though remembering Carponti was present, shook himself.

"So, I need to borrow your camera, sir." It felt weird calling Trent 'sir'. They'd served together in Germany when Carponti had been a private and Trent had been his platoon leader. Carponti, for one, was grateful that Trent was his commander. Carponti doubted he'd have gotten away with half the stunts he'd pulled had it been some other pencil neck officer in charge.

Trent frowned and sat down at his desk. "Can I ask why?"

Carponti grinned. "You may not really want to know the answer to that question. But I'll tell you if you really want to know."

"Let's just stop there while I can still cherish my innocence." Trent shook his head and kicked his feet up onto his desk. "Change of subject away from your delinquency. How's Iaconelli working out?"

Carponti thought about the booze and then decided he really didn't give a shit. Iaconelli wasn't getting drunk, which meant he was a functioning alcoholic at the very least. So long as he kept performing and keeping the guys out of the hospital, Carponti couldn't really argue the means. There was enough shit going on that he didn't need to get the commander spun up on that. Not when LT Randall was out of control and they were potentially missing optics. "He's not Sarn't G, that's for sure."

"Not many people could step into Garrison's shoes."

Carponti frowned. "Well, that would be gross. Do

you know what kind of fungus is growing around here?"

Trent pushed his glasses up onto the top of his head and leaned back. He didn't laugh. Carponti took that as a very bad sign. "So listen. There's some bad shit going on."

"And you're telling me something I don't already know because...?" Carponti said. He tapped his fingers on the butt of his weapon.

"Look, I know you took Garrison getting hit hard but there are other things going on. If I get pulled out of this job, I need you to keep things running smoothly, okay?"

Carponti looked at the rank on his chest and ignored the thousands of questions skipping through his brain, about why his commander might get fired and why he was talking to one of his squad leaders about it. "You realize I'm a buck sergeant, right? As in, pretty low on the list of people you should expect to run things if you're not here. And where are you going, anyway?"

"I'm not going anywhere if I can help it." Trent swung his feet to the floor and leaned forward on the desk. "You've got influence, whether you see it or not. The guys look to you to gauge whether shit is really bad. If you're still around cracking jokes, then everyone else tends to just keep rolling along."

Carponti held up his hands. "Obviously you've been drinking too much coffee because you're a little intense right now. Why would you get fired?"

"It's a long story that requires a significant amount of alcohol." He glanced at his computer. "You're heading home on R&R in a few days, right?"

"I wanted to talk to you about that." Carponti

shifted in his chair uncomfortably. He wanted nothing more than to go home and see his wife and forget about the war for a few days but the feeling of dread that gripped his insides turned the thought of leaving his boys for the holidays into something sour. It felt like he was abandoning them. And as badly as he needed to connect with his wife, with as badly as he needed to know she was still there for him, he...he couldn't bring himself to leave. Not with everything going to shit around them.

Nicole would kill him if he didn't come home. Goddamn, he knew how hard this Christmas was going to be for her. It was breaking his heart to even think about asking to skip his R&R but his guys were having too hard of a time right then. God, but he hoped she'd understand. "I don't think it's a good time to go. The guys are still off kilter from Sarn't G getting blown up and all and well..."

Trent held up one hand. "You're going," Trent said flatly.

Carponti looked up.

"You're going. As much as you like to think you are, you're not the Energizer Bunny. You need to take a knee and unwind just like the rest of us."

Carponti frowned and started to argue but the small piece of fabric in his pocket was suddenly heavy. It was a stupid thing, this desire to tease his wife with a picture of a stupid costume but suddenly, he very much wanted to do it in person. He wanted to watch her double over in laughter. He wanted to feel her laugh when he was inside her. There was nothing better in the world than hearing her laugh. Nothing better than feeling her body tremble when he touched her.

The pressing need for the camera flittered away. He could show her the man dress in person in a few more days.

He swallowed and nodded. "I get that. I don't like it but I get it."

Trent opened his mouth to say something, then paused before he spoke again. "You're not going to argue?"

"Nah. There's something I really want to give my wife. I was going to send her a picture but I can do it in a couple of days when I get home."

A strange look passed over Trent's face. "Yeah, you need to take care of her. Don't let her forget you."

"When is the last time you talked to Laura?" Carponti asked quietly.

Trent shook his head and reached to turn on his computer. "Just...when you go home, if you see my wife..." He bit his lip and Carponti had never seen his friend more unsteady in all the years he'd known him. "Tell my wife I love her?"

Carponti wanted to press Trent on what the hell was going on but the phone rang and Trent waved him out of the office. Things had gone to hell in a relatively short period of time. Garrison had gotten blown up, Trent was missing equipment and potentially facing an investigation...and the rumors... The rumor mill was breeding faster than a barn full of unsupervised bunnies.

He was suddenly glad he'd be getting on a plane and heading home soon. Carponti slipped from the tactical operations cell and headed back to the bay to prep for the next mission. One last mission before he got to see his wife.

❄ 9 ❄

"So we're going to provide the blocking force here and here," Iaconelli said, drawing an x in the sand. "This intersection that sits squarely in a bad part of town."

Carponti reached for the stick before Iaconelli could snatch it out of his hands. "And by bad part of town, Sarn't Ike means the locals would rather slit your throat than feed you to the dogs. Which is pretty bad, all things considered."

Iaconelli snatched the stick out of Carponti's hand and looked like he wanted to beat Carponti with it, completely unimpressed by Carponti's sarcasm. Carponti scowled. He must be losing his touch.

"Someone hasn't had their daily pick me up," Carponti grumbled. A couple of the guys laughed until Iaconelli glared at them.

"The enemy has been very active in this sector," Iaconelli said, ignoring Carponti's jab.

"And we know this because every time we roll

through this sector, we get blown up," Carponti added.

"Are you trying to piss me off?" Iaconelli snapped.

Carponti looked up. "Is it working?"

"Yes."

"Then yes."

A few more chuckles from the guys. Iaconelli pointed toward the door. "Outside, funny guy."

Carponti bowed as he exited in front of his platoon sergeant. The guys heckled as Iaconelli practically shoved Carponti through the door. Carponti spat into the dirt and waited. They were all just trying to survive and Iaconelli was making it fucking miserable.

"You need to quit screwing around before you get someone hurt."

It took a lot to piss Carponti off. Like, act of God to really get him going, but right then, Iaconelli's words shot straight to the heart of his temper. Iaconelli was bigger than him by about a half a foot and seventy-five pounds, but well, Carponti had never really thought his actions through.

He shoved his platoon sergeant back against the bay doors with a bang. "Considering you've probably been drinking since before the sun came up, I don't really think you get to lecture me on doing something stupid that might get someone hurt," he said quietly.

Iaconelli broke Carponti's hold easily and shoved him backward. "You don't know shit about me, you little smart-ass."

"Really? You want to play that game? I make

jokes to keep the guys from getting too fucking depressed. In case you haven't noticed in your alcohol-induced fog, we've had a pretty shitty deployment. If a joke makes them think about something else, then maybe, just maybe, I'll keep them from focusing on all the bad shit. But I wouldn't expect you to notice that because your coping mechanism is at the bottom of a bottle."

Iaconelli grabbed Carponti by the front of his shirt and cocked his fist back. Carponti puckered his lips up and made a kissing noise. "You only get one shot," he taunted.

Iaconelli pulled back and Carponti realized perhaps this wasn't his smartest move.

Iaconelli swore and shoved him away. Carponti stumbled backward but kept his feet, then smirked and made a show of straightening his uniform. "And so we've reached an impasse. Shall we continue with the war? The one outside the gates, I mean."

Iaconelli jabbed a finger in Carponti's face then bunched his fist and said nothing. He stalked back into the bay.

Carponti spat into the dirt again and followed him back in, threw his arms around Iaconelli's shoulders and grinned. "Yes, yes, boys, we kissed and made up. Now back to your regularly scheduled war."

Iaconelli shrugged him off roughly but otherwise ignored him as he moved on with the mission brief. Carponti wished he could blame the lingering adrenaline from the near fight with Iaconelli but as they rolled out the gate, he couldn't shake the feeling that bad shit was coming. And when Iaconelli insisted on changing up the vehicle locations so that his truck was in front of Carponti's, the bad feeling got progressively worse.

But he kept that to himself. Because he was just being paranoid. Right?

He listened to the radio as they rolled out deep into insurgent territory. Everyone was on high alert.

He tugged on Tigger's leg, reminding him to duck down behind the defilade. Too many soldiers had gotten beheaded from wires strung beneath intersections and across roadways. Garrison had driven that point home more than once.

They passed the soccer stadium without incident and Carponti nearly pissed himself with relief. They were heading toward the Iraqi police station where they were supposed to link up with their Iraqi Army counterparts.

Providing they made it there without getting blown all to—

The blast shattered the windshield on his truck. A moment later, a cloud of dust and debris rolled through the interior. Instantly, Tigger and the other gun trucks started laying down suppressive fire. When the dust finally cleared, he saw Iaconelli's truck lying on its side.

Oh fuck. If they hadn't changed up the order of movement, that would have been Carponti's truck lying there in the dirt. Shit, he'd known that was a bad idea.

"Holy shit," he muttered. "Tigger, keep suppressive fire going. Wilks, Jax, I need you with me to get them out of that truck before they get blown all to shit."

It was a horrible case of *deja vu*: rushing across the road just like he had with Garrison. He climbed onto the truck and managed to yank the door open.

Inside, Iaconelli and the boys were coughing but everyone looked unhurt. "You girls okay?" Carponti shouted over the chaos.

Iaconelli flipped him off.

"Nice to see you, too, sweetheart." Carponti ducked as a rocket whizzed overhead, grossly off target. God, but he was happy the insurgents had crappy aim. "Y'all want to get your asses out of there? Kind of a hot zone out here."

The driver and gunner climbed out, followed last by Iaconelli. Iaconelli paused in the doorway.

"You're never serious, are you?" Iaconelli asked.

"I thought we already had this conversation."

Iaconelli heaved himself out of the truck. "We need to try to get this thing back on all four wheels."

"Got it covered." The Humvee in front of them was already maneuvering into position to try and drag the flipped truck over. More rounds tinked off the truck's armor and Carponti ducked down behind the door he was still holding. "Shit, that one was close."

"Get off the damn truck before you get blown up," Iaconelli said, leaning over the side of the truck and firing at a group of approaching men armed with what looked like a couple of rocket-propelled grenades.

"Oh goody, the greeting committee," Carponti mumbled.

"Get down!"

It was the last thing Carponti heard.

"Carponti!"

The voice came from very far away. Carponti frowned and tried to open his eyes. They were heavy. Something was burning.

"I hope that's not my balls," he mumbled.

"Jesus, you never stop. Open your damn eyes."

"Am I still in Kansas?" Carponti frowned and managed to blink. His vision cleared slowly and Iaconelli came into view, clearly not happy. "What's that smell?"

Iaconelli glanced at Carponti's side, then his gaze flicked back to Carponti's face. "Don't worry about it."

"Wait, that smell is me?" Panic clutched at him, closing off his lungs.

"I said don't worry about it. We've got the MEDEVAC coming for you."

Carponti tried to sit up and Iaconelli damn near flattened him with a single palm to the chest. He groaned. The pressure made him see spots. "Oh, what the hell? Did I manage to get myself blown up?"

"Little bit."

A slow ache sharpened abruptly, tearing up his arm and down his side like molten fire. "Oh, now I feel it," Carponti said. He no longer tried to sit up. The fire in his arm went from nonexistent to eleven in less than a nanosecond. He winced and breathed out hard. "That stings."

Iaconelli cleared his throat as he continued to do whatever he was doing to Carponti's arm. "Yeah, I'm sure it does."

Carponti reached up with the hand that didn't feel like absolute hell and gripped Iaconelli's body armor. "Give it to me straight. Just tell me if my dick is still intact?"

Iaconelli flushed and finally laughed. "I have no idea and I'm not checking for you."

"Jesus, it takes me getting blown all to hell to get you to laugh? That is seriously fucked up."

He wasn't a fan of the gory details. But he had to know. "Dude, seriously? I can't move my arm to check myself."

Iaconelli's gaze flicked over to Carponti's side again and the source of the pain. Carponti was tempted to look, he really was. But he knew something bad had happened. Nicole was going to be so pissed at him.

"You're fine. Does that help?"

Carponti sulked. The thunder of overhead air support rumbled closer. "Not really, but it looks like my ride is here." He frowned and bit down on his lip as a bolt of pain ripped through his arm and down his side. "Is it bad?" he finally asked Iaconelli as the helo touched down. Dust swirled violently around them. Moments later, he was jolted onto a stretcher. "Ow."

"The docs are gonna sort you out, okay? But I think it's a long way from your heart."

Carponti managed to laugh. "My dad used to say that to me all the time." He blinked and looked up at Iaconelli. "Does that make you my daddy?"

"Fuck off, Carponti," Iaconelli growled. But for once, he didn't sound like he wanted to knock Carponti's teeth out.

Which Carponti took as a very bad sign.

⁂

HER PHONE RANG AT FIVE THIRTY IN THE MORNING. Nicole was instantly awake, praying it was Vic. "Hello?"

"It's Laura. I need help."

An hour later, Nicole was busy in the emergency room, trying to help Laura keep order in the chaos. Laura's call for help with the Family Readiness Group had been desperate. Someone had leaked on social media that their unit had wounded soldiers coming in from Germany and everyone was gossiping and trying to figure out who was hurt. Normally families would have already been notified if their loved one had been wounded but this was the Surge and nothing was normal anymore. It had happened more than once that soldiers had been wounded and shipped halfway around the world before families had been notified.

Today, apparently, was turning into one of those days when getting a manifest was in the too hard to do category.

The emergency room was crowded full of spouses jockeying for information, and the staff there was doing their best in the middle of abject insanity. Nicole fought for patience as she tried to herd the women and two men into some semblance of order while she waited for Laura to figure out what was going on. She breathed deeply and tried to keep her own fear from paralyzing her.

There was no news from Vic. No e-mail telling her

he was okay. No phone call. Fear clutched at her heart as she tried not to hover near Laura and their friend Jen—a nurse at the hospital—who was trying to get the list of names of the wounded from the admin folks.

She almost missed her cell phone vibrating in her pocket. She fumbled for it and nearly dropped it before desperately connecting the call.

"Hey, babe."

Nicole almost collapsed with relief. "You're okay," she breathed. "You're okay."

"Yeah, about that." She froze. Her heart stopped in her chest. "Um, I'm kind of in Germany."

Tears instantly burned behind her eyes, pouring down her cheeks. She swiped at her face. "What? Vic, what's going on?"

He breathed deeply on the phone. "So, I got blown up a little bit." He cleared his throat. "I'm going in for another surgery so I'll call you when I'm out." His voice was strained.

"How bad?"

"I'll see you when they evac me back to the States, okay?"

"My ass you will. I'm getting on a plane." Like hell she was going to sit there and wait. They didn't have a ton of money but her mom could get her a flight. Nicole knew her mom would do that much.

"Nic—"

"Don't argue. I'm coming."

He didn't say anything for a long moment. His silence terrified her but she held it in. "Okay." He paused. "I love you."

Her voice cracked and broke. A flood of fear

crashed against her heart. "I love you, too. I'll be there as soon as I can."

She hung up the phone. Laura was right there. Nicole's eyes burned. "Vic's been hurt."

"What can I do?"

"I'm good. I've got to go, okay?" She was this close to falling apart. She needed to get away from the pitying looks from the wives who'd overheard the conversation.

The wives who were grateful it wasn't them. She couldn't blame them. It came with the territory. It was a guilty relief, a terrified fear that maybe next time it might be their loved one.

Right now, none of that mattered. She needed a plane ticket now. She didn't have time to fall apart.

Laura pulled her into a quick hug. "He's okay."

"I know." Nicole wiped beneath her eyes. "I'll let you know as soon as I know something, okay?"

Laura nodded and let her go.

Nicole was on the phone instantly, having her mom make the travel arrangements. She packed a bag in a blur. Somehow she remembered to pack a coat. She didn't even check any luggage. The plane took forever to taxi down the runway.

Her thoughts raced. Her heart drummed in her ears. She didn't do well with sitting on her hands but there was nothing else she could do. She paid the flight attendant for three little bottles of vodka. The first one burned all the way down then spread through her veins like a languid, numbing balm. The second one made her head fuzzy. She pulled the dark blue airplane blanket over her chest and turned her face toward the window so no one would see the tears as they ran down her face.

The third one went down smooth and she forced her eyes closed. She didn't sleep. She couldn't stop the fear that ate at her. Vic was in the hospital. He was alive. She clung to that thought amongst all the chaos in her head on the long hours of the flight to Frankfurt.

Her husband was alive. Whatever else happened, he was alive.

❧ 10 ❧

It was dark the next time the puffy cloud of morphine let him go. He blinked and tried to open his eyes but they were still too heavy. So he lay there in the dark and waited for the drugs to fade a little more.

He had a vague memory of being sent out of Iraq. The flight on the hospital plane was nothing but noise as far as he could remember.

He frowned as he blinked, hoping his eyes would obey at some point in this century. There was an itch on the palm of his right hand that was driving him crazy. He tried his hand to rub his fingers together to scratch it and felt...nothing.

Going in for surgery.

Carponti swallowed hard against the snippet of memory and breathed deep against the panic in his chest. *Oh fuck.*

He didn't burst awake in a panic. He blinked a couple of times then opened his eyes. Another deep, unsteady breath and he held up both hands. There was empty space where his right hand should have been. His forearm was heavy and numb and wrapped in thick gauze.

His eyes burned. *Oh fuck. Oh fuck.*

He covered his mouth with his hand. His hand. He held it up. His left hand was intact. He made a fist. His fingers closed. Okay. Wedding ring. He needed to find it. Nicole was going to kill him.

He looked at his right hand. Or, rather, the space where his right hand used to be.

The bandage was thick and heavy and extended past his elbow to his mid upper arm. He felt like his hand was still there but the empty space his eyes saw argued with the sensation in his brain.

Alone in his room, Carponti didn't have any smart-ass comments. He couldn't really come up with anything funny to make himself laugh.

He just kind of sat there for a minute and did nothing.

He didn't swear at God. Or get angry.

He just... sat.

It was much harder to wrap his brain around his missing hand than anything else. He was going to have to learn to write with his left hand. Was he still going to be able to shoot? Hell, he was going to have to learn to fire left-handed.

He scrubbed his left hand over his mouth. He stopped looking at the bandage and the empty space. Echoes from before his surgery came back to him.

Infection. We have to amputate now.

Might lose the whole arm if we don't.

He swallowed. All of that was a blur. He remembered making a crack about his balls but maybe he hadn't because the doctors hadn't laughed.

Maybe his sense of humor had been in his right hand and that had been amputated, too.

That was a shitty feeling. Holy crap, Nicole was going to be pissed. Had he called her? He couldn't remember if he'd called her.

What if she freaked out about it? What if she took one look at the missing appendage and executed an about face and walked out of his life forever and went and found someone who was still a whole person? Someone who hadn't left her alone for years on end while he was off fighting some stupid ass war.

A man with both his hands to hold her with.

Holy hell, he didn't want to call her. He wasn't ready for that. She was going to be so pissed at him for getting hurt. Damn it, how the hell had he gotten himself blown all to hell in the first place? He frowned and glanced down at the bandage. *Residual limb.* Was that what it was called? Where had he heard that?

The silence was closing in on him. He wondered if the nurses would be irritated if he got out of bed. He didn't do well with sitting still. Never had. Hell, he'd driven his teachers nuts when he'd been a kid. The ginger kid with the smart mouth. He'd made everyone laugh. Except his teachers. They had never been amused.

He had a sudden, terrified thought that maybe he was missing more than just a hand. He froze.

Took a deep breath and lifted the blanket.

His legs were intact. A white bandage spread across his hip. Oh fuck. He lifted the gown.

Relief was something cold and wet that slapped across his skin. Everything was still there. His arm buzzed like a low jolt of electricity that hummed over his skin. He lifted it back onto the pillow where it had been resting before he'd started fidgeting.

He had to piss. He could do that by himself, right? He pushed the blanket off his legs. Hospital gowns were so sexy. He cradled his bandaged arm against his chest and gently eased his legs over the edge of his bed.

His head spun and the world tilted. He gripped the edge of the bed for a moment, waiting for the spinning to stop.

There was a quiet knock on the door. His stomach pitched, imagining Nurse Ratchet coming in to give him hell for getting out of bed.

The door to his room swung open.

And a thousand emotions crashed into him.

His wife stood in the doorway, a small bag over her shoulder. She looked rumpled and tired and so goddamned wonderful. His heart did a funny flip in his chest. Right above the bandaged limb he'd cradled against his hospital gown.

NICOLE STOOD THERE, ROOTED TO THE SPOT. HE HADN'T shaved. There was at least three days of stubble on his face. A light dusting of red hair. His cheeks were thinner. He hadn't been eating well.

But his hair had grown back.

Tears burned behind her eyes. She felt like she hadn't stopped crying since she'd left the States.

She stood there—her husband a dozen feet away —and she couldn't move. He looked so good. So tired. So strained.

Her gaze drifted down his body, stopping on the bandages wrapped around his right arm. And reminded herself to breathe.

⚜

His first urge was to hide his arm. To keep her from seeing what had happened to him.

To run and hide from the fear of her reaction. The worst fear in the world seized him: that she would turn around and walk out that door. Asking her to wait for him had been nothing compared to this: asking her to love him when he was missing a piece of himself.

A thousand options raced through his head. Fear burned through him. He'd be damned if he was going to cry about it. So he sat a little straighter, despite the dizziness that threatened to pitch him face first onto the floor. And wouldn't that be a disaster?

"Hey, babe." His voice sounded strange to his ears. "Don't be mad. I got a little blown up."

She bit her lips together. Her eyes filled. Fear stabbed him in the heart. She was going to leave. She was going to leave. Oh fuck, she was going to leave.

She dropped her bag and rushed to the bed. It was all he could do to move his bandaged arm out of the way.

And then she was there, her face pressed to his neck, her arms tight around him. A shudder rocketed through her. Grief, happiness, sorrow. A thousand emotions ripped through him, tearing at his heart and blocking his throat.

He froze for a moment, not really believing that

she was there, in his arms. For the first time in months, he was holding his wife.

And at that moment, nothing else mattered. Not the missing hand. Not the months he'd spent away.

He wrapped his arm around her and held her tight. Breathed in the scent of her hair. Savored the feel of her body against his. "I'm sorry," he whispered. "I'm so sorry."

And when she crawled into the bed with him, he didn't argue. He held her as best he could and tried not to embarrass himself by crying.

***

Nicole came awake slowly, the steady beat of her husband's heart warm beneath her cheek. She lay there for a long moment, just feeling him breathe, reassuring herself that yes, this was real.

It was morning. She'd fallen asleep after the doctor had come in and brought her up to speed on Vic's injuries and where he stood. Vic's expression when the doctor had said no sex would have been almost comical if the warning hadn't been so serious. She'd spent the rest of the evening lying with her husband, reading through the pamphlets the doctor had left. She remembered lying there quietly when the nurse came in to take his vital signs.

Her fingers curled over his heart as the tears threatened again. She wasn't normally this much of a crier. At least, she hadn't been before this deployment. It was just fatigue. She'd get some more rest and then she'd be fine.

Vic was alive. She sniffed quietly, trying not to

wake him, but his arm tightened around her shoulders.

"Hey," he whispered.

"Sorry." She swiped at her eyes. "I didn't mean to wake you."

He pressed his lips to her forehead and she closed her eyes as the sensation of him touching her warmed her terrified heart. "You didn't," he said.

She swallowed and wiped her eyes, not wanting to move from the cocoon of warmth in his bed. She vaguely remembered the nurse asking her to sleep in the chair. She wasn't sure if Vic had threatened the woman but she knew she'd been allowed to stay.

"Are you hungry?" she asked.

"They already brought breakfast."

She turned her head, and saw the tray sitting off to one side. She brushed her hair out of her face and looked down at him. He looked tired. But he'd never looked better to her. "What time is it?"

"After eight in the morning." He reached up and brushed his fingers over her cheek. "You slept a long time."

"Sorry," she mumbled.

His lips were curled in a funny half smile. "Don't be."

Her stomach rumbled and he smiled. "Eat, if you're hungry."

She looked at him and tipped her chin. "Did you eat?"

Vic shrugged. "Haven't had much of an appetite."

"They're not worried about you not eating?" She sat up, crossing her legs and sitting on the edge of the bed. She felt fuzzy, like she needed a shower. But she didn't want to leave him. It was a stupid fear but she was terrified to let him out of her sight.

"I'll eat if I get hungry." He reached for the tray and pulled it closer. "You eat. I'm good."

She lifted the pale plastic lid of the domed tray. "Wow." Three pieces of French toast, two slices of bacon, and two hard-boiled eggs. She frowned, then immediately changed the direction of her thoughts.

Vic caught her. "What?" he asked.

She hesitated, hating herself for being so unsure around the man who'd always made her laugh. "I was just thinking the hard-boiled eggs were kind of messed up to give to a guy with only one hand."

Vic blinked for a long moment then busted out laughing. He reached for her, pulling her close as he laughed. She smiled and wiped at her eyes.

"You scared me," she said softly. She swallowed. "The next time, can you give me a little more information than *Hey, babe, I got blown up?*"

"Well, I...wasn't really sure what to say. I'm usually not at a loss for words and...well, yeah." He held up his bandaged arm.

Her expression softened. "Does it hurt?"

Carponti snorted. "No. They've got me on so much morphine right now they could probably cut off my other hand and I wouldn't feel anything." He held up his good hand. "Not that I want to test that theory or anything."

Nicole smiled. And his wife, his beautiful wife, cupped his face in her hands and kissed him.

WITH ONE KISS, SHE BANISHED ANY AWKWARDNESS HE'D

imagined between them. He didn't want it to be awkward. He wanted his wife to curl into bed with him and... Well, the doc had said he wasn't authorized to have sex yet but that didn't stop his imagination.

She ran her fingers over his cheeks. Something so simple. He closed his eyes and let the tingling sensation run through him.

She cupped his face and he was conscious of the fact that his jaw was covered with bushy red stubble. "But you're okay. And that's what matters."

He just sat for a moment and looked at her. Savored the feel of her hands on his body, even if it was just his face. She was touching him. She was here and she hadn't run screaming from the room at the sight of his bandaged hand. He covered her forearm with his good hand. Her skin was warm and soft and real beneath his.

He was suddenly really glad she wasn't a drug-induced hallucination. "I can't believe you got on a plane that quickly."

She smiled. "It was a long flight." Her fingers drifted over his cheek.

She was touching him. She wasn't horrified by the missing hand. His thoughts kept repeating, over and over. Fear made him still, prevented him from reaching for her and pulling her close again. He was afraid. Afraid she was in shock. Afraid she was still adjusting to the idea of his missing appendage.

Missing body parts were a big adjustment, or so he'd been told. There weren't any briefings that could prepare you or your spouse for this. At least, none that he'd attended before. Maybe there were now.

Nicole looked away and slipped her hands from his face. The loss of her touch physically hurt him.

But he didn't say anything. Because he didn't have the words to bring her back.

She started sorting through the bag of things that had apparently come in with him from Iraq. He had no idea what was in that bag, but he wasn't entirely sure she should be going through it. He didn't want her stumbling across a bloody uniform or worse.

She pulled a small plastic bag out and held it up. His dog tags glittered muted silver in the fluorescent light along with his missing wedding ring. She pulled out his wallet and a clump of fabric. Carponti flushed and said nothing.

Somehow, his sewing project didn't seem funny right then.

"I'm glad you're here," he whispered, holding out his hand for the baggie. He took a deep breath, then dumped the contents onto his lap. His dog tags jingled against his wedding ring. He maneuvered the plain gold band onto his finger, then managed to use his thumb and pinky to get it back where it belonged.

Nicole hadn't noticed but it was a small victory for him. It felt right having his ring on. She turned back toward him, her lips curled faintly. "You didn't honestly expect me to sit in Texas and wait for you, did you?"

"I don't know. We never really talked about something like this."

She glanced down at his bandaged arm, then pushed the tray out of the way and climbed over his legs until she straddled him. And just like that, any chasm he'd imagined between them was gone and Carponti was lost in the sensation of his wife's body against his in all the right places. Okay, maybe not *all* the right places, but close enough.

"So listen," she said, crawling up his body until her knees rested on either side of his ribs. "This sucks but it's not the end of the world."

"You're going to get in trouble with the nurses," he said. He rubbed his hand over her hip, urging her a little closer.

"Since when do you care about following the rules?" She smiled and rocked against him even as she slid her arms around his neck. "I missed you so much, Vic."

The block of fear around his heart melted and thawed.

"So the good news is that everything from the waist down is still intact." He smiled wickedly up at her. "Want to take it for a test run?"

She rocked against him gently and cupped his face in her hands. "I'm sure we'll figure it out," she whispered against his mouth. "But no sex until after the wound is healed. I'm not violating any doctor's orders and risking you getting sick."

Carponti pouted. "Seriously?"

Nicole wrapped her arms around him and nestled closer, a laugh shaking through her body and into his. Laughing with him was almost as good as sex. Okay, not really, but it felt so damn *normal.* "Not until the docs give you the green light."

Carponti angled his body and pushed the nurse's button before Nicole could stop him. "Can I help you?" The nurse's voice was scratchy over the speaker.

"Yeah, I need a note from the doctor so I can have sex with my wife."

"Vic!" She tried to snatch the handset.

"Um, I'm sorry, sir. Can you repeat that?"

"Sorry, ma'am." Nicole grabbed the button. "Ignore him. He's high. We're sorry, ma'am."

She put the button out of reach, then snuggled up to his side. "That poor nurse," she said, laughing quietly.

"I'm serious." He rolled toward her and cupped her face. "I missed you." He swept his hand down her side. "All of you."

"I missed you, too. But no sex until the doctor says so."

Carponti sighed dramatically. "You're no fun."

"It's only a little longer."

"I have to be careful for the first few weeks so the wound can heal. Are you honestly telling me we're going to wait *weeks*?" Carponti pouted for a second and then blurted, "Oh shit."

"What?" Nicole was instantly alert. "What's wrong?"

Carponti lifted his bandaged hand. "This was my right hand."

"Yeah?"

"I, ah...pursue certain pleasurable activities with my right hand. Now I've got to learn to do it with my left."

Nicole buried her face in his shoulder and laughed. "There's something so wrong with you." But her voice broke and a shudder ran through her.

The emotions snapped inside him as her tears wet the hospital gown. He held her close and let her cry, so goddamned grateful that he was there to hold her. The thought of her crying on his grave threatened to choke him. "I'm okay, babe. I'm okay."

"I know." She leaned up and sniffed, wiping her eyes. "I just... I'm just glad you're here. I don't care about anything else. You're here. You're okay."

"I mean, I'd rather be elsewhere—"

She slapped his chest gently. "You know what I mean."

He smiled. "Yeah. I know what you mean."

He held her for a while. The noise from outside the hospital room faded away and he fell into sleep, holding the one person in the world who mattered most to him.

H e woke up to a gentle kiss on the side of his mouth. He turned and nuzzled his wife. The doctors didn't like her sleeping in the bed with him but he didn't actually care. For every night over the last week, she'd waited until the late night nurse had completed her rounds and then she'd crawled into bed with him, careful not to bump his arm.

He slept better when she was with him. Her weight against his side was comforting and solid and real.

She'd stayed with him and he counted his blessings every single morning when he woke up and she was there. "Good morning," she whispered, nestling closer.

"Morning." He kissed the top of her forehead, savoring the quiet warmth of her body against his.

As hospitals went, Landstuhl Medical Center was pretty good. Food wasn't bad, nurses were nice when they weren't irritated with Carponti's antics.

The door opened and Nicole tensed. Carponti's arm tightened around her to keep her from leaving the hospital bed.

"You're going to get in trouble," she whispered.

"Don't care."

The doctor walked in. Carponti grinned. "Good morning, Doctor Kevorkian."

The doctor's face flushed red beneath his white hair. He did not look amused. "My name is Doctor Goldstein, sergeant. I've told you that about six times."

"Well, yeah, I heard you the first five times. But Doctor Kevorkian has such a nice ring to it."

Nicole was crying in hysterics next to him, trying to catch a breath to talk.

His wife's hand shot up to cover his lips. He kept talking but it was muffled beneath her palm. "Just ignore him," she said. She looked up at him. "Stop before you give the man a heart attack."

Carponti turned his wide-eyed expression on his wife. "What?"

Nicole's face was lit up with a brilliant smile. "The doctor does not share your sense of humor. What can we do for you, sir?"

The doctor's flush retreated a little bit with the knowledge that at least one person in the room wasn't clinically insane. "Looks like we're going to release you."

Carponti stilled. Nicole dropped her hand from his mouth and slipped from his embrace.

"Okay." She climbed out of the bed and pulled on a sweater and paid close attention to what the doctor said. She asked questions Carponti didn't hear over the loud buzzing in his ears.

Somehow, things had reached stasis in the hospital room. He felt safe here. He'd learned to get his pants down with one hand. Started getting used to the idea that he was suddenly left- handed. But now? Now this was like jumping out of the airplane without a parachute. Being released? He wasn't ready to face the world. Not like this. Would people stare? Yeah, they'd stare. Hell, he'd stared every time he saw someone with a missing limb. He'd felt like an ass doing it but it was just so...different.

And now he was about to be released into the wild? He wasn't ready for that.

The doctor left and Nicole turned, a stack of papers in her hands. "They're going to bring all your medication up so we don't have to wait in the pharmacy," she said softly. Concern was written all over her face and he loved her for it.

But Carponti couldn't find a single thing to say.

⚜

SHE WASN'T USED TO HER HUSBAND BEING QUIET. Before, when her normal had included mundane tasks like getting groceries and paying bills, she'd always assumed her husband's silence meant he was getting into something. Mischief and all that. Now? Now a new silence emanated from him and she was not used to it at all.

She read over the discharge paperwork, watching him out of the corner of her eye. He sat on the edge of the bed, his back to her. His head was down, his shoulders slumped.

She didn't think he was getting ready for a joke.

She set the paperwork down and climbed over the bed. She slipped behind him and dropped her legs around his hips then wrapped her arms around his waist. She simply sat there, leaned against him, and said nothing. Hoping that her actions were enough because she wasn't sure she could say anything without the tears breaking through again.

After a long moment, he leaned back against her, his hand sliding over her forearm.

"It's going to be okay," she whispered when she was sure her voice wouldn't crack.

"I know."

"But?"

He paused for a long time, his thumb rubbing along her skin. "I don't have any pants. I am positive that if I go strolling around the medical center in my gown, I will give at least six sergeant majors a heart attack."

She laughed then and, this time, tears didn't come. She laughed and simply held on to her husband because he was okay. He was a little shaken up, a little unsteady but he was okay. If she kept telling herself that often enough, maybe she'd start to believe it.

"I can go to the PX and buy you some clothes."

"Just pick me up some sweatpants, okay? Nothing fancy with buttons or anything?"

She crawled around and stood in front of him, her arms draped around his neck. "What's that supposed to mean?"

"It means you always dress like a million bucks and you'll probably find some very uncomfortable, starchy clothes that will make me itchy."

"You're always itchy in real clothes. It's like you have an aversion to them."

He grinned. "I do. Dress pants are a lot harder to get off when we're getting ready to do the horizontal tango." He held up his bandaged arm. He slid his hand down her side, resting it on her hip, and urged her close to nibble on her lips. "You have no idea how turned on I am," he murmured against her mouth.

Her throat went dry. She wanted very badly to kiss him. To feel his mouth on hers, his tongue slide against hers. But she was terrified that if she did, she wouldn't be able to stop.

And there was a fear, nestled deep inside her, that he wasn't as okay as he was pretending to be. And she'd be damned if she was going to do anything that would risk getting him hurt or sick or keep him in the hospital any longer than he'd already been here.

"Me, too," she whispered. "But doctor's orders."

He made a growling sound deep in his throat. "I'm going to find someone with the first name Doctor to write me a note." He stroked his hand over her hip and tiny bolts of electricity hummed through her. God, but she missed him.

"I'm going to go buy you some clothes before I do something stupid," she said, slipping out of his arms.

"Define 'something stupid'?" he asked, his eyes glittering in the fluorescent light.

"Stupid as in lifting up that all too sexy hospital gown and riding you off into the sunset."

"Oh, I definitely think we should do something stupid." She scooted off the bed before he could grab her. "Not funny," he said.

"It's a little funny."

He lifted said hospital gown, revealing a very healthy erection. Nicole's body ached for him. She released a shuddering breath. "We can't, honey."

"First I lose a limb and now you're going to leave me like this? What kind of wife are you?"

She laughed and finished getting dressed. She palmed her wallet and her phone and paused. "So do you, ah, want to go home right away?" She looked up at him, watching his expression carefully.

"Do you?"

He glanced down at his bandaged arm. "I don't know. I mean, we're already here and we always talked about coming to Europe. I suppose we could travel a little bit before going home?"

She tipped her head and studied him. "Are you up for that?"

"I mean, I'm not skiing the Matterhorn any time soon but there's no reason why we can't ride the trains around Germany for the holidays, right?"

There was something in his voice, something that whispered to her that he wasn't cracking any jokes. She leaned in quickly and kissed him lightly. "I'll be back in a little bit."

"I'll be here. Learning a new skill."

She paused by the door. "Huh?"

"Learning how to masturbate with my left hand."

She laughed and ducked out of the hospital room before he lured her back to that far-too- tempting bed. He was making jokes.

It was a good sign.

CARPONTI STOOD IN THE MIDDLE OF THE HOSPITAL ROOM in fuzzy new blue sweatpants and a t- shirt. The new shoes were rigid on his feet but they'd break in easily enough. It felt strange, being in real clothes again. Even stranger when he forgot to reach for something with his left hand because he kept forgetting that his right was no longer there.

There was a tingling in his phantom limb but he could manage it. He wasn't due for his medication for a while longer. But the pitch in his stomach had nothing to do with the medication or lack of food.

He was fucking scared. Scared of facing the world and the staring eyes and the stolen glances full of unspoken relief that it wasn't them.

His wife's arms came around him from behind and he covered her hands with his one.

"You okay?" she asked. Her voice vibrated through his back.

"Yeah," he said lightly, hiding the panic twisting inside him. "So it looks like I'm on convalescent leave for oh, the rest of the year." He turned and pulled her close. "When do you have to be back at work?"

She tipped her head up and wrapped her arms around his waist. "I've got the greatest boss in the world. She told me to take my time."

He held her close, loving the feel of her body against his. He brushed his lips against her hair, hoping this celibacy was going to end soon. But it was enough, for now, that she was here and things were as normal as they would ever be again. "So I was serious about going sightseeing around Germany for the holidays. There's a little town down south called Rothenberg Ob Der Tauber one of the nurses told me about. Supposedly it's like this little

Christmas village and stuff." He shrugged. "Since—well, I kind of didn't make it home for Christmas—maybe this will make up for it."

She slipped her arms around his neck, brushing her lips against his. "You made it home just fine."

"Just not in one piece."

She shook her head, her lips curled in a faint smile. "None of that matters. You're home. You're safe. There's no better gift for Christmas." She kissed him then and he thought to hell with the doctor's orders and kissed her back.

He lost himself in the feel and taste of his wife. The beauty of her faith in him and the solid feel of her love.

He had her.

Nothing else mattered.

She eased back.

"I swear to God I'm going to kill the doctor," Carponti growled, lowering his forehead to hers.

His wife laughed and brushed her nose against his. "You ready to face the world?"

"Not really," he said honestly. "I've already got two strikes against me and now I'm missing a hand. I'll never be in the cool kids club again."

She frowned. "I have no idea what you're talking about."

"I'm already a ginger kid with a smart mouth. Now I'm short one appendage? Oh yeah, I'm going to be the life of the party," he mumbled.

She kissed him gently. "You'll always be the life of the party with me."

"Hopefully that will be a private party really soon," he grumbled.

She laughed against his mouth then rested her

cheek against his.

Carponti held on to the relief that sighed against his heart.

The Bavarian countryside sped by as the train rolled through the evening. There hadn't been snow when they'd been further north in Frankfurt, but as they traveled south in Bavaria, snow capped the roofs in traditional German villages and bright Christmas lights illuminated houses against the darkness that fell as they traveled.

Nicole watched the hills roll by, amazed by the pockets of villages and hamlets that dotted the countryside. And trees. There were so many trees. Not miles and miles of suburbs or highways. Just beautiful countryside lit up like a Christmas card. It was nothing like where they lived in the States, with thousands of strip malls that looked exactly the same on every corner.

Beside her, Vic's head bobbed and he yanked it up.

"Hey," she whispered.

"Hmm?"

"Lay your head in my lap," she whispered. "Sleep."

He didn't argue. They shifted around so he could keep his bandaged arm elevated and then he rested his head on her thigh. It was a comfortable weight and she ran her fingers over his hair and rested them on his neck. His pulse beat steady and strong beneath her fingertips, in time with the rumbling of the train over the tracks. The rhythm was steady. Comforting.

His hair had grown. It was longer and thicker than she'd ever seen it. He still hadn't shaved. She'd thought about offering to shave him but hadn't. She was worried about how to handle his new normal. Did she offer to help? Leave him be? She didn't know. But she'd gotten slowly used to the idea of her husband and his new beard. He looked rugged and sexy, but she couldn't tell him that.

He'd try to seduce her in the rail car and while she was always up for an adventure, she didn't really feel like getting arrested by the *polizei*. Spending Christmas in a German jail was not on her bucket list.

She'd fired off a few e-mails before they'd left the hospital wifi, but otherwise her phone was currently useless unless she wanted to pay ridiculously high overseas charges.

Besides, she didn't really need to know what was going on in the outside world. Not really.

She brushed her fingers over Vic's hair. His breathing was steady and low. He'd fallen into a deep sleep.

He was trying so hard to act like everything was normal. And a large part of things *were* normal. She hadn't expected that. Not after something like this.

But it was still a shock, getting used to the

missing space where his hand used to be. She'd catch him looking at it every so often, and then he'd make some kind of joke and deflect her concern away. But she knew. She wouldn't call him on it but she was going to watch him carefully.

He was okay. Mostly. But that didn't mean she wasn't still worried.

He shifted against her thigh. She rested her head back against the seat and closed her eyes against the tears that threatened.

He was okay.

It was all that mattered.

🕉

THE VILLAGE OF ROTHENBERG WAS SOMETHING OUT OF A Christmas filmmaker's dream, nestled inside an old walled city. It glowed against the starlit sky, full of beautiful gold and silver Christmas lights. Massive Christmas trees, decorated with classic German ornaments, stood in the central squares and brightly lit, festive shops were overflowing with shoppers. The cobblestone walkways glistened with ice as the heat from the day's sunlight faded, and the moisture on them started to freeze after the sun disappeared into the west.

They walked through the gates and into the walled city down the main *strasse*. The air was crisp, biting at their exposed skin. His arm was starting to throb but he took another pill and buried the pain. It was bad enough he'd landed in the hospital without a hand, but he didn't even have a Christmas present for his wife. He wasn't going to ruin their pseudo vacation by being a wuss about the pain.

It was just a missing limb. He still had three other ones.

Carponti walked with his wife down the narrow streets, past the ancient buildings and clock shops. Christmas was everywhere. Christmas trees—*tannenbaums*—and Santa Claus figurines were stacked on tables as people wandered by. Everything was slower here. People didn't rush, even though it was Christmas Eve.

They stopped by a tent and bought *gluhwein* and bratwursts.

"How are you feeling?" she asked as she squirted dark brown mustard on the bratwurst for him.

"Can you take the napkin off?" he asked. "Don't feel like eating paper and wrestling with it."

He glanced over at a little kid poking his head out behind his mother's wide hips. The kid couldn't have been more than seven or eight. His eyes were glued to Carponti's bandaged arm.

Slowly, the child lifted a finger. *"Was is das?"* His mother looked down, then followed the direction of her son's gaze. Horror spread across her face rapidly and she yanked her son's hand down. *"Entschuldigen."*

Carponti looked at his wife as the mother hurried off with her child, scolding him in sharp German. "Well, parental mortification looks the same in any language," he said dryly.

"I suppose that's going to take some getting used to," she said quietly.

"What, getting stared at?" Carponti said. He stroked his hand over his beard. "Why wouldn't people stare at a sexy beast like me?" he asked with a grin.

Nicole smiled but his joke fell flat. "I think it'll get easier," she said, her hand on his chest.

"Yeah." He brushed his lips against her forehead. "I'm sure it will." But he didn't sound convinced. "Maybe I should get a puppet for it or something."

They ate quietly for a few minutes. Nicole didn't say anything and he watched her as she ate her brat.

It was a damn good brat. First real food he'd had since before he'd left for Iraq. The chow halls over there were pretty good, all things considered, but there was nothing like a freshly grilled bratwurst.

Carponti set his brat down and tugged her napkin from her. He ran it slowly over her cheek, catching the tiny spot she'd missed. He loved the way her lips parted, her breath freezing in a huff. "Think we should try to find the *gasthaus?*" he asked.

A huge Christmas tree lit up the square behind her. She was framed in soft light. There was moisture on her eyelashes.

He loved that he could still touch her. She nuzzled her cheek against his palm. "I think that sounds good," she whispered. "I want to run into one of these shops and try to find a restroom."

He didn't move. Neither did she. He stroked his thumb over her flushed cheek. Standing in the fading winter night, Carponti kissed her. A gentle kiss. Conscious of his beard hurting her, he parted her lips with his. He felt her quick intake of breath, her palm on his chest to steady herself.

This. Oh God, but he'd missed this. Her tongue slid against his, reminding him of everything he'd missed, everything he'd longed for while he'd been gone.

Everything he'd been terrified he'd never feel again.

Nicole opened herself to the hesitant caress of his gentle touch. She sighed and swayed against him, bracing herself as a floodgate opened wide and unleashed a torrent of desire.

Their lips broke apart with a gentle suction. He lowered his forehead to hers. "I've missed you so much," she whispered.

He closed his eyes, unable to speak, unwilling to break the moment with something crass. With one single kiss, she'd nearly dropped him to his knees.

"I really need to find a guy named Doctor," he muttered against her lips.

There was nothing sweeter than the sound of her laughter. In front of that tree, he wrapped his arms around her and simply held her.

❧

THE SUN CREPT INTO THEIR TINY ROOM AT THE *GASTHAUS* early the next morning. The window was covered with frost, sending soft rays of light into the room.

Carponti shifted and pulled Nicole tighter against him, rolling until she was entwined with him. Her thighs were tangled in his; his good arm wrapped around her shoulders. He rested his bandaged arm on his hip, keeping it elevated and away from being bumped. At some point, he was supposed to start toughening up the tissue to start prepping for a prosthetic but he wasn't there yet.

Nicole made a sleepy sound in her throat and nestled closer. He lay there, on Christmas morning and was simply...still.

It took a lot for him to be still. He closed his eyes and breathed in the smell of her shampoo, the scent of her skin. His eyes burned and he blinked hard a few times, not believing that this was real.

Never in his life had he thought this day would come. A day where he held on to his wife with one arm because a piece of the other one had been sacrificed to the gods of war. He thought about Garrison. He needed to get an update on him asap. It dawned on him that he had no clue what had happened to his boss. Maybe Nicole would know. He'd have to remember to ask her later.

He wondered how the platoon was doing without him. Captain Davila hadn't been doing well before that last explosion. He was worried about him but there wasn't a damn thing he could do about that now.

Nicole shifted in his arms and he realized she was awake. He brushed his lips across her forehead and she lifted her mouth to his. "Merry Christmas," she whispered.

"I got you something," he said. He untangled himself from her and sat up, reaching under the bed for a small bag.

"When did you have time to do that?"

"When you ducked into that shop to find a bathroom." He was proud of the fact that despite everything that had happened, he'd still managed to get her a gift. It was small but he kind of thought she'd like it. He twisted, bending one knee in front of him before he handed it to her. "Didn't have time to wrap it, though. You didn't take nearly enough time in the bathroom."

She smiled and shook her head before taking the

bag from him. "I wasn't in the bathroom. I got you something, too."

"Sneaky woman."

"Well, you can't use it for a while." She handed him a small box.

He fussed with the bag until he got the box out of it, then managed to get the top of the box open. It was slightly smaller than a shoebox. "What the heck is it?"

He pushed back the tissue paper and pulled out a German beer *stein*. It was a large mug with a pewter lid, decorated with a scene from the village in Rothenberg in a wild splash of reds and blues and creams. A thick lump rose in his throat when he saw the date scrawled on the largest building. December 25, 2007. He looked up at his wife.

"So we'll always remember this Christmas," she said quietly.

Carponti sniffed and said nothing for a long moment, simply staring at the mug in his hand. Nicole shifted closer, sliding one hand onto his knee and tipping his face to meet hers.

"You made it home," she whispered. "I know it's not how we thought it would happen but you're here. And I will always cherish this Christmas as the one when you came home to me."

Carponti swallowed the lump in his throat and blinked back the burn behind his eyes. "Damn it, there's something in my eyes." He swiped at them, stuffing down the storm of emotions inside. He handed her the small bag he'd hidden beneath the bed. "Open it?"

It was a silly thing he'd bought her. It had been on a whim but he thought she'd laugh. Now, after the stein, he wasn't so sure. The morning felt more somber. More real. Hell, this vacation wouldn't have happened if not for the explosion.

He watched her intently as she opened the first of two boxes. She pulled out the small globe and held it up in front of her face. Inside the globe was a space for a photo. "I figured you could put a picture of your dad in it," he said quietly.

She offered a watery smile as she leaned in and pressed her lips to his. "It's beautiful. I love it."

"Open the next one."

She narrowed her eyes. Damn it, she'd heard the funny note in his voice. He had to get better at hiding things from her. Or maybe not.

She set the next box on her lap and lifted the lid. "What is it?"

"Look closely."

"Oh my god, Vic, you didn't."

It was a tiny piece of cloth. Nicole covered her mouth with her hand and laughed hysterically. "Is this what I think it is?"

"That depends on what you think it is," he said carefully.

"Man dress?" Tears welled in her eyes and spilled down her cheeks as she laughed. She was still laughing as she crawled into his lap and kissed him.

"I take it you like it," he said.

"You have a sick sense of humor but yes, I like it." She kissed him until he was breathless and the sadness he'd felt a moment before dissipated in the love of her touch. "I love it. Did you actually make it yourself?"

He smiled, loving the fact that his wife was in his lap.

"Merry Christmas?" he said.

Her laugh bubbled up, warming his heart and so much more. She wrapped one arm around his neck while she slipped her hand down the front of his pants. "Cute. How long did that take you? And when can we try it on you?"

She slid her hand down the length of him and a shudder tore through him. "Jesus, that feels good," he whispered.

Arousal, hot and needy, pulsed through him as she stroked him.

She kissed him, her hand sliding up and down his length slowly. "I don't want to wait anymore," she whispered.

"Thank God."

He started to lift her shirt. "Let me," she said.

She pulled her long-sleeved t-shirt over her head, gently easing it up, teasing him with every inch of exposed flesh before pushing his pants down over his hips.

He tugged at her bra and she reached behind her to unhook it. His hand on her breast felt so good. Like a piece of her had been missing until that very moment, that single touch that lit her entire body on fire.

She moaned when he gently took one nipple between his teeth. "Oh god, I missed you," she murmured, holding his mouth to her.

She rocked against him, felt his erection rubbing against the seam of her pants. "You're wearing far too many clothes," he said.

"I can fix that." She stripped off the rest of her clothes then crawled back into his lap, pushing him down onto the bed.

His body was hot beneath hers, his hair crisp against her inner thighs. She loved the rough feel of him beneath her. She rocked against his erection, savoring the feel of that first touch.

"Honey, I hate to tell you this but I'm not going to last long."

"I don't care." She kissed him then and angled his erection to just there at the entrance of her body. She rocked gently and he hissed between clenched teeth. She bit his bottom lip.

Then she slid down his length, taking him deep.

Taking him home.

Her throat closed off. She buried her face in his neck for a moment, unable to process the intense emotion of having him there, inside her, around her.

With her.

His arms wrapped tightly around her. The bandage on his arm was rough against her back. She didn't care. She didn't care because everything else was real and hot and good. So goddamned good.

She started to move, to rock gently over him. His expression tightened. His body tensed.

And then she felt him coming, deep, deep inside her. Touching the last reserve of her soul.

Reminding her that happiness—her happiness—was with this man.

"Sorry," he mumbled against her neck.

"Oh, I'm sure you'll take proper care of me later," she whispered, still rocking against him, her own pleasure there, just there.

He slipped his hand between their bodies, finding her swollen and aching. He fumbled with his touch. His face flushed but she leaned back, giving him space, letting him learn how to touch her body all over again.

He touched his wife, their bodies still connected. He stroked her just right and she clenched around him, rocked against him. Made the tiny sexy sounds that he'd missed so goddamned much while he'd been gone.

She rocked hard against him, her pleasure exploding, squeezing his still hard body deep inside her. She buried her face in his neck as it rocketed over her and sent them both tumbling into the abyss.

He held his wife close and fought back tears that burned behind his eyes. Her arms were tight around him, her breath hot against his bare skin.

Now, he was finally home.

It didn't matter where they were.

He'd made it. Maybe not all of him, but he'd made it. Safe and warm in his wife's arms, he'd made it.

He was home.

Thank you for reading **I'LL BE HOME FOR CHRISTMAS**. I hope you enjoyed Carponti and Nicole and their Christmas homecoming.

Keep reading to find out what a broken hero will do win back the woman he loves. Find out what happens in **BACK TO YOU**.

Trent has given his life to the Army. When he faces his darkest challenge, it will take the love of a strong woman to get him on his feet again and dare him to love again. Can Laura forgive him for leaving her alone for so many years

One click BACK TO YOU, a sensual second chance romance now!

EXCERPT FROM BACK TO YOU

Prologue

Fort Hood
2007

"I put your checkbook in the front pocket of your ruck sack. Did you find the sleep medication? You'll need to sleep on the plane so that you're rested when you land. And I put your calling card—"

Captain Trent Davila looked up from where he sat on the edge of their bathtub. He held a tiny folded flag in his hands. For a moment, he'd been somewhere else. Sulfur scorched the inside of his nose. The thunder of the fifty cal reverberated off his breastbone.

"What's that?" she asked softly, watching him from the bathroom door.

He held out his palm so she could see the little flag. "Good luck charm. I can't deploy without it."

A thousand questions flickered over her face as

her gaze fell onto that tiny flag. She bit her lip and turned away, but not before he saw the naked fear looking back at him.

He moved, stepping in front of his wife and capturing her face in his palms. Her skin was smooth and soft and achingly familiar, and a deep part of his soul missed her already.

But that part of his soul wasn't in control right now. The moment she touched him, his soul recoiled, refusing to let him take even the simplest pleasure in her touch.

He'd cheated death and he knew, *knew* he didn't deserve to be there with his wife when so many of his men had died.

That's why he had to leave. Again. It didn't matter to where. It didn't matter if it was the war in Iraq or a transition team somewhere in the mountains of Afghanistan. He needed to get away. To get back into the fight.

And pray that his wife would understand why he had to go.

"Laura." He whispered her name, capturing her attention.

She tried to look away, to pretend that today was just another day. But Trent knew her too well. He saw the doubt and the fear that she tried to hide. Her eyes, though, her eyes always gave her away. He stroked an errant strand of copper hair away from her forehead, meeting her golden eyes, unable to speak any words of comfort. He knew they'd just be more empty lies.

She offered a watery smile. "I'm terrified of losing you again," she whispered.

"I've deployed since I got hurt. This time is no different."

"You didn't get hurt." She refused to meet his gaze. "You died. Your heart actually stopped beating. And this time is worse. This is the Surge." Her voice broke. "I can't lose you again," she whispered. Her voice cracked as the tears tumbled down her cheeks.

He hated to see her cry. Worse, he knew he could prevent those tears.

He pulled her close and simply held her, wishing he could feel as alive with his wife and family as he did when he was at war. Maybe someday, when the war was over, he could figure out what had broken inside him and how to fix it.

He stroked his thumbs over her cheeks as the kids shrieked in Ethan's bedroom. The sound sent a spike of anxiety through Trent's heart, but he smiled, hoping to cheer her up. "Sounds like someone just lost a Lego."

"Daddy!"

"He's probably going to beg you for a hamster again," she said. Laura swiped at her eyes, blinking rapidly. "Can't let them see me like this."

He slid from her embrace, regret sealing the walls that four deployments had erected around his heart. Trent tried not to notice how intently Laura watched him, her gaze sweeping over the scars on his body as he finished getting dressed. His dog tags banged against his ribs as he dragged his t-shirt over his head and pulled on the rest of his uniform and then his boots.

"Well, you could get one," Trent said, needing the distraction of simple conversation.

"Or," Laura said with a smile that didn't reach her

eyes, "you could promise him one when you get home. It'll give him something to look forward to."

Trent frowned at the odd note in Laura's voice and focused on tying his boots and tucking the laces beneath the cuff of his pants. "He won't even notice I'm gone. They're both too little."

Trent straightened as Laura approached, placing her palm over the scar on his heart. It burned where she touched him. It took everything he had not to flinch away from the gentleness in that touch. "Keep telling yourself that," she said with a soft kiss. "They miss you when you're gone. We all do."

He sighed quietly and glanced at her, resting his hands gently on her hips. "Laura, you know I have to go."

He couldn't explain it. Didn't have the words to explain the emptiness inside him that consumed every waking moment when he wasn't over there. And worse, he didn't ever want her to see the emptiness he tried so hard to hide from her.

She believed he'd come home. As long as she continued to believe that, his world would continue to exist.

She brushed her thumb over his bottom lip. She blinked rapidly and the sight of her tears almost penetrated the cold empty space where his heart had been. "I just wish it got a little easier waiting for you, that's all." Her fingers wrapped around his dog tags, her thumb sliding along the chain. "But we'll be here when you get back. We always are."

He ran his fingers lightly over her face. The lie he'd told his wife so often sat like a concrete wall between them. She didn't know that he'd volunteered for this deployment, for so many others, and he had no way of killing the lie without killing their marriage. "Don't go getting a deployment boyfriend while I'm gone."

"I don't think you have to worry about that." Laura wrapped her arms around him, nuzzling his neck. They stood for a long moment before Laura eased away.

Trent swallowed and let her go. Again.

❧

FIVE HOURS LATER, TRENT KISSED HIS WIFE GOOD-BYE for the fourth time in six years. His four- year-old son and two-year-old daughter were getting antsy, climbing up and down the bleachers non-stop. As he walked away from the gym where he and the rest of his unit had checked in for the deployment, he glanced up at her in the stands. She was steady. Stoic. Trying valiantly not to join the ranks of the wives and children who were crying as their soldiers left them, assault packs and weapons in hand. God but he wished he didn't have to go. That he was man enough to stay home and fix whatever was broken inside him. Wished that he were man enough to need her more than the heady, uncertain terror of war.

"You ready, sir?"

Trent glanced over at First Sarn't Roy Story, a man who'd taught Trent the right way to kick in doors and the difference between knowing when to wipe a nose or whip an ass. The war was lined into Story's leathery face. Fifteen years as an infantryman that had started in Mogadishu and continued with the long slog through Iraq.

"Are we ever really ready for this?" Trent asked,

taking one more long look at his wife and kids. And then he turned away, needing to harden his heart for the battles to come.

Outside, Trent climbed aboard the bus that would take them to the airfield. Spouses filed out from the gym along the sidewalk. In the seat behind him, Sergeant Vic Carponti was harassing one of Trent's platoon sergeants, Sergeant First Class Shane Garrison. He almost smiled. With those two around, things would never be dull.

He scanned the crowd, searching for his wife amongst the blurry faces of other people's spouses lining the sidewalk. There. She held her vigil in front of a light pole, a tiny hand in each of hers. Beside her, Ethan stood bravely, tears streaming down his face. He held a tiny salute, his mouth pressed into a flat line as he tried to be a tough little man. Emma waved brightly at the bus, still too little to fully understand that Daddy was leaving for longer than a trip to the grocery store.

He looked away but it was far, far too late. When he closed his eyes, the image of his small family was seared onto his retinas as the bus pulled out of the parking lot and headed for the airfield.

"Never gets any easier, does it?" Story asked quietly, sucking on the end of an unlit cigar while he fiddled with a light on his helmet. There was little love left between Story and his wife. Story deployed to avoid his wife.

But Trent deployed to avoid his *life*. Because life back in the rear was too complicated, too loud, too chaotic. War was simpler.

The scar on his chest ached and he rubbed it,

wishing he could forget the way his family looked as the bus pulled away.

He closed his eyes, trying to put them out of his mind. He didn't want to remember his wife with her cheeks streaked with tears or the raw grief in her eyes. He wanted to remember her face as she slept curled into his side. Or laughing with their kids. He needed to carry those memories into war with him. Because that was all that would steel him against the long hours and bone-crushing fatigue to come.

He had soldiers to command. His family would be there when he came home.

He hoped.

Chapter One

Fort Irwin,
California 2008
One year later...

Trent walked out of the ops tent, needing a few minutes to himself. They'd just sent word that the wife of a kid in one of the companies was in the hospital. She was going into labor while her husband was enjoying the fun and sun of the National Training Center.

At least the kid wasn't deployed. He'd be able to get home quickly. Sure, not as quickly as if he was back at Fort Hood, but still. It beat the hell out of trying to get home from Iraq.

The notification was something simple, and yet it had struck Trent that yet another soldier was going to miss the birth of his child because of the Army.

He knew exactly how that felt and right then, a

thousand bitter memories rose up, reminding him of everything he'd willingly squandered. The resurrected hurt was so raw, the regret so powerful, he nearly choked on it.

He should be used to the hurt by now, but lately it seemed to be getting worse. It overwhelmed the dead space inside him, forcing him to feel things he didn't want—and wasn't ready to feel.

He didn't know *how* to feel them, how to deal with them. So for the moment, he sat outside the ops tent and let the raging emotions storm inside him. Until he could get them under control. Until he could function again.

It had been happening more and more this year. The things he'd stuffed away had started having a nasty habit of reappearing when he least expected them.

He was starting to get comfortable with the crazy, but at least now he was starting to recognize the warning signs. Which was why he was sitting outside the ops tent.

"So your BFF Marshall is looking for you." Story walked out of the ops tent, a smirk on his face that only meant bad things for Trent. It was so strange calling him "master sergeant" instead of "first sergeant" but Story wasn't a first sergeant anymore. Just like Trent was no longer a commander.

Trent sat on the hood of a Humvee, smoking a cigar and contemplating his sixth cup of coffee since he'd come on shift twelve hours ago. He pushed his glasses up higher on his nose then glanced over as Story hopped up next to him.

Since they'd both been fired more than a year ago, they'd been hanging out on the staff together, responsible for nothing but PowerPoint slides. Funny how getting fired meant giving up the hard jobs in the Army. You still got to stay in the Army, but you just weren't trusted with taking care of soldiers anymore. It was a punishment, being put in the easy jobs. Trent would have given anything to get his old job as a company commander back, but that wasn't going to happen so he and Story and Iaconelli kept each other sane and avoided the new commander. Captain James T. Marshall the Third drove everyone fucking crazy.

"Should I be worried?" Trent asked dryly, adjusting his glasses again. He'd long ago given up getting upset when Marshall attempted to piss in his corn flakes. Marshall had been tapped to take over Trent's company when he'd gotten himself fired and Marshall took great pleasure in reminding everyone that he was fixing all the things that Trent had screwed up. It grated on Trent's last nerve every time the words, "Well, sir, I'm still fixing the mess I was left when I took over" came out of Marshall's mouth at staff meetings, but what could Trent say? He *had* gotten fired. It didn't matter why. He supposed part of his penance for being a shitty commander was having to listen to Marshall without knocking his teeth out. He'd leave that for Story and a few of the captains, like Ben Teague, who were leading the insurgency on the staff. Trent had other things on his mind.

Like his wife. His two kids. The house that was no longer his.

He cleared his throat and tried to listen to Story.

"I don't know," Story said. "Marshall wasn't screaming so I think maybe you should be okay?"

Sergeant First Class Reza Iaconelli, one of Trent's former platoon sergeants, stepped out of the ops tent. "No, you should definitely hide," he said, interrupting the conversation. "He's bitching about having to transport you back to the rear early and he's pretty cranky."

Iaconelli was a big man: broad shoulders and built like an ox. He was steadfast and solid downrange but when they got home? Yeah, that's when things went to shit for Iaconelli. He'd never met a bottle of alcohol that he didn't like. He was lucky he still had a career but the sergeant major liked him. Trent respected his ability in combat enough to overlook any personal failings. Trent was the last one to judge someone's personal failings.

He reined his thoughts back to the present and the feeling that flittered in the dead space around his heart. "I'm getting sent back?"

Iaconelli shrugged. "Maybe they're finally going to court-martial your sorry ass," he said

lightly.

Trent flipped him off. "That would be nice, actually. If they'd at least get the damn thing

over with. If I never see Lieutenant Jason Randall ever again, it will be too soon.

"He is a special little fuckstick, that is for certain," Iaconelli said, staring at the end of his cigar for a moment.

Iaconelli may or may not have threatened to kill LT Randall downrange. Twice. But all of Randall's interpersonal hostility had been a sideshow, a distraction to keep Trent or anyone else from figuring out that he had been selling sensitive items and funneling the money to bribe the Iraqis to stop blowing their boys up. Randall had finally gotten caught and now was determined to take down Trent and anyone else he could with him. Iaconelli chopped the tip off his cigar and sucked on the end while he tried to light it.

"Too bad I won't be around for his court-martial," Story said.

"Did you get reassigned?" Iaconelli asked Story.

"Yeah. I'm deploying again in about two weeks. As soon as we get back from here," he said.

"Your wife isn't going to be happy," Trent said quietly.

"Actually, she's going to be thrilled. It'll give her a chance to find her some twenty-year- old boy toy to keep her busy while I'm gone." Story spat into the dust.

"So you're still married because...?" Iaconelli sucked on the end of his cigar.

"Because it's too fucking expensive to get divorced," Story said. "I'll take care of it after this next deployment. I'll save up some money first, though."

"Sure you will," Trent said. "You've been saying that since '04."

It was Story's turn to flip Trent off. "At least I'm willing to accept my marriage is over."

Trent rubbed his heart, knowing his first sergeant hadn't meant to score such a direct hit. At least, not with malice. "Yeah well, my divorce is complicated."

"These things always are." Iaconelli leaned against the truck. "Which is why I've never gotten married."

Trent snorted and was going to make a crack but Marshall took that opportunity to step into the darkness outside the ops tent. "Davila, you're going back to Fort Hood."

Trent glanced at his watch. "It's four thirty in the morning."

"And you're going to be on a plane in three hours. Pack your shit." Marshall turned to stalk off, mumbling about pain in the ass captains and not having enough time for this shit.

Iaconelli blew a smoke ring into the darkness. "God but he is such a charmer."

Trent sat there long after Story and Iaconelli went back into the ops tent.

He wanted to go home. But now that it was happening, fear slithered down his spine.

It had started slow. One day, he'd wake up, dreaming about Laura. Other times, he'd be in the mess tent and he'd think he heard her laugh. He'd hear a kid giggling on the TV and he'd look up, expecting to see Ethan or Emma.

Always, though, he was alone. He'd wanted it that way for so long. He'd wanted quiet when they'd been running around his feet, shrieking and bickering like kids did. He'd craved silence at the end of the day when someone would get out of bed for a glass of water.

He'd certainly gotten the silence and the solitude.

And the oppressive emptiness of it all ate away at him. He'd thrown himself into work here in the California desert. He'd pulled eighteen hour days gladly. The longer he spent away from the war, the less he felt its siren call, luring him back. And somehow, work wasn't enough anymore. Nothing he did pushed away the aching need to get to the one place he simply didn't belong: home.

He was back in the States but he couldn't go home. Not with an investigation hanging over his head and the potential for a very long jail sentence standing in front of him. And the worst part about the entire court-martial was that his brigade commander was changing command soon. If Colonel Richter left before the case was resolved, Trent would be at the mercy of the new commander—a new man with no loyalty to the soldiers he'd put in leadership positions.

It was not a comfortable place to be. The power plays between the senior officers never ended well for junior officers, and Trent? Trent was caught right now. He had to trust that Colonel Richter would take care of this before he left.

But a year after Trent had been sent home, Trent was running low on trust and patience.

Patience had never been his strong suit. Every other time he'd been home, he'd been prepping to go back to war. This time, the year had stretched in front of him like an unending slog.

It was the longest time he'd spent in the States since he'd gotten shot. It had taken him almost that long to realize just how badly he'd fucked up everything in his life that was supposed to be important.

His marriage. His kids. His family.

If there was a grade lower than an F at being a husband or a dad, he'd earned it. He'd come home from Iraq nearly a year ago—pending a court-martial and a divorce. And since then, nothing had happened. The case had been stuck in investigation mode forever. And the divorce? He just wasn't able to sign the papers. His life had been frozen in carbonite on all counts.

The investigation had moved slower than molasses in winter. And he was glad.

Because standing out here in the California desert, he'd come to a conclusion. He wanted his family back. He wanted his *wife* back. When she'd slapped him with divorce papers last year, he'd refused to sign them, hoping that the investigation would go away and that he could fix things with her. But that hope had proved futile. The distance between them was too much. The warmth he remembered was gone, but still, he'd been unable to let her go. He couldn't. Sure, they spoke on the phone or when he saw her at the office, but they were a few stolen minutes here, a quick chat about the kids. There was nothing there to give him hope that he could fix things with her.

He'd volunteered to train soldiers anywhere he could so that he didn't have to face the cold emptiness of the reality that he was no longer welcome in his own home. And if he volunteered, someone else wouldn't have to.

Now? Now he sat in the middle of the California desert and thought about the new dad who wouldn't be there for the birth of his child. He looked down at his wedding ring and thought of all the time he'd willingly given up.

He was a goddamned fool. He wanted her back. Damn it, he wanted his *life* back. The life with this woman who had once smiled and laughed with him and wrapped herself around him while she slept. Who was as beautiful changing Emma's diaper as she was dressed up in an evening gown for the Cav ball. This woman who used to ask about his day when he called home at two in the morning, even after she'd been up half the night with one of the kids.

He sobered, his hands trembling at the thought of his children and the tiny family that had grown while he'd been away. The tiny family that overwhelmed him and terrified him and dropped him to his knees with a need so strong, it crushed his lungs until he could not breathe.

He didn't know how to feel good, but he knew he'd never figure it out without them.

He had no clue where to start. He had no idea how to be a father to his kids. Or a husband

to a wife who could barely look at him.

Trent hopped off the top of the truck. He had a phone call to make.

Because it looked like he was getting exactly what he wanted.

And it was time to figure out how to be the man his family needed him to be.

❧

FORT HOOD

"Son of a bi-iscuit!"

"Bad Mommy!"

Laura Davila wrapped her scraped and bleeding knuckles in a paper towel and prayed to the patron saint of Army wives for patience. Her six-year-old dishwasher was currently spread in carefully laid out pieces across the kitchen floor and counters. And now the cavernous white interior was splattered with her blood. Awesome.

Her son Ethan looked up at her with disapproval

in his dark brown eyes, and Laura flinched. "Sorry, honey. Mommy just hurt herself."

"You said a bad word." This from her daughter, Emma. "Agent Chaos said you're not allowed to say those words."

Laura glared at the fat brown hamster that was clutched in her daughter's hands. Agent Chaos looked up at her with disapproving beady brown eyes. Sitting there, silently judging her.

She had joked with Trent that he should buy the kids a hamster when he returned from his latest deployment. By the time he came back, things between them had already crumbled but he still remembered the damn hamster. He'd bought not one, but two of the stinking, smelly creatures. The hamster cuteness factor did not override the pain in the ass factor of having to clean their cages every other day to keep the smell from overpowering the entire house.

Maybe if Trent had been around more over the last year, she wouldn't have minded them so much. But instead of sitting at Fort Hood and working in an office like any other officer who was under investigation, he'd volunteered for several rotations at the National Training Center in Fort Irwin. He'd spent more time there than at Fort Hood over the last year. He might as well have just moved there.

She took a deep breath and pressed on her throbbing knuckles, focusing on the pain so that she wouldn't feel the tension that squeezed her heart every time she thought about her husband. She regretted sending him the divorce papers. She could admit that now, but she'd done the only thing she could at the time.

She could still remember that stupid flare of hope when he'd stood in her office that day. Hope that maybe, finally, he had come home to her.

But he hadn't.

And as time had ticked by and he'd refused to sign the papers and let her go, she'd moved beyond regret. Now, she wanted to move on with her life. Maybe someday she'd be able to think of Trent without the hurt and frustration that kept reminding her of everything she'd lost.

"You have to pay us each a quarter," Ethan said, stroking the fat orange hamster in his hands. Laura was seriously thinking about buying a cat—that would solve the hamster problem quickly enough. But it would be just one more thing to clean up after.

And she wasn't really up for the trauma of finding a dead hamster under the bed.

She could only imagine the therapy bills.

She pursed her lips and counted to ten...thousand. "Okay, guys, why don't you go play in the garage or something? Mommy has too many parts in here, and I don't want you to get hurt."

Or move anything. But she didn't say that out loud, because that would only encourage them to run off with some vital component that it would take her three days to identify and two more days to find online and order. A new dishwasher was not in the budget at the moment. Besides, she wanted to see if she could actually fix the thing herself.

She shooed the kids and their accompanying hamsters out of the kitchen and made her way through the master bedroom to the cache of Band-Aids she hid in her bathroom. The kids were all too eager to use every bandage in the house if she let them, which always meant that she couldn't find a Band-Aid when she really needed one. She'd resorted to hiding them like they were some kind of precious commodity. In her house, they were.

Laura pulled down the shoebox that held the first aid kit. She held her breath as she cleaned the cuts on her knuckles with iodine, then wrapped gauze halfway down her fingers, covering the empty space where her wedding and engagement ring had once been.

She paused, staring at her ring finger. Blood pooled on the pale band of skin there, as if her finger refused to forget the rings that had been there since forever.

Her finger might not forget the rings but that didn't mean it was a marriage worth waiting for. No amount of waiting or wishful thinking was going to change that. Trent had seen to that. And broken her heart all over again.

She knew in her heart that they were finished. He had lied to her so many times about his deployments. That alone had destroyed her trust in him. And then there was the rest of it...

She was ready for the pain to stop. Ready for her heart to stop waiting for the phone to ring. Waiting, so desperately, for her heart to stop beating for a man who was never coming home.

A spike of melancholy pressed on her lungs. Damn it, what was wrong with her today? She was past mourning the death of her marriage. At least, she kept telling herself that. So when was it going to stop hurting?

She briefly considered a shot of vodka to numb the pain, but that wasn't really a good idea since she was alone with the kids. She barely ever had a drink these days. She sighed and glanced wistfully at the discreet box on the top shelf in the bathroom closet. Droughts were not limited to alcohol.

She had gotten used to it, this new normal. While the kids were vibrant chaos, full of life and joy, the married part of her life was... well, it simply was. There was nothing there anymore. No joy. No hatred. Just silence and cold detachment overlying a dull aching sadness.

She simply wanted it to be over. And damn Trent to hell for dragging it out when he wasn't even willing to fight for them. And the silence between them? Between her and the man she'd thought she'd love for the rest of her life?

She sat on the edge of their bed, one finger rubbing absently over the bruised knuckles and her empty ring finger. She could hear the kids shrieking in the garage. One of the hamsters had gotten away. She smiled. She really didn't mind them, not when the kids loved the judgmental little beasts so much. It was a gesture of kindness from a man who couldn't be a father. She knew that.

It didn't make it hurt any less. She'd married him knowing what she was getting into, thinking her love for him was strong enough to withstand whatever the Army could throw at them. Knowing that the Army was a demanding job, that he'd be gone a lot. But that first deployment had done something to him, something deeper than just the visible scars on his body.

Once, she never would have thought the silence would grow too loud or that his empty side of the bed would become too heavy to bear. Once, she would have waited forever for him to come home to her.

But forever was a long time.

And her faith in their love had died long ago on some distant battlefield.

ONE CLICK BACK TO YOU NOW!

ACKNOWLEDGMENTS

This book was probably the most fun I've had writing in a long, long time, and first and foremost I have to thank my readers for clamoring for Carponti ever since the scruffy sergeant first hit the page. I hope you enjoy his story as much as I enjoyed writing it.

As with all my projects, it takes a village. First, I have to thank my agent extraordinaire Donna Bagdasarian for believing in me and being there when the poo and the fan were making babies. You don't know how much your support and faith means to me. To Amy Pierpont, thank you for proving there is still loyalty in the world. Paula Robinson, thank you for keeping me straight on series continuity! Finally to my talented editor Michele Bidelspach, thank you for seeing the potential in these stories and helping me write them the way they needed to be written.

And to my family. We're off on a new adventure

but most importantly, we're off on it together. I'm so eternally grateful that Mommy and Daddy are home for Christmas.

BOOKSHOTS

Dawn's Early Light

Author's Note

The Coming Home series and Homefront series were originally published as separate series. I have rebranded them to get things organized as they were originally intended.

Come Home to Me: A Coming Home Novella* was originally published as part of the Homefront series

Carry Me Home* was originally published as Until There Was You as part of the Coming Home series

A Place Called Home* was originally published as All for You as part of the Coming Home series

Take Me Home* was originally published as It's Always Been You as part of the Coming Home series

Last One Home* was originally published as Find My Way Home as part of the Homefront series

Jessica Scott is an Iraq war veteran, an active duty Army officer and the USA Today bestselling author of novels set in the heart of America's Army. She is the mother of two daughters, too many animals, and wife to a retired NCO.

She's also written for the New York Times At War Blog, PBS Point of View Regarding War, and IAVA. She deployed to Iraq in 2009 as part of Operation Iraqi Freedom (OIF)/New Dawn and has had the honor of serving as a company commander at Fort Hood, Texas twice.

She holds a Ph.D. from Duke in sociology and

she's been featured as one of Esquire Magazine's Americans of the Year for 2012.

Photo: Courtesy of Buzz Covington Photography
Find her online at http://www.jessicascott.net

For more information,
www.jessicascott.net
jessica@jessicascott.net

9 781942 102984